THE GUNSMITH

460

The Traveling Undertaker

**Books by J.R. Roberts
(Robert J. Randisi)**

The Gunsmith series

Lady Gunsmith series

Angel Eyes series

Tracker series

Mountain Jack Pike series

COMING SOON!

The Gunsmith
461 – Standoff in Labyrinth

For more information visit:
www.SpeakingVolumes.us

THE GUNSMITH

460

The Traveling Undertaker

· J.R. Roberts

SPEAKING VOLUMES, LLC
NAPLES, FLORIDA
2020

The Traveling Undertaker

ISBN 978-1-64540-260-2

Chapter One

Caleb Wellington had purchased his wagon from an elixir salesman because he needed the kind with walls and a door he could lock for safety. He had also bought this particular one because it was longer than most. For his business he needed more room inside than a normal medicine wagon offered.

The wagon was drawn by two Clydesdales, one grey, one brown. He preferred them because of their strength and stamina, for his business required him to haul heavy materials. He hoped the horses would last him some time without having to be replaced, as they weren't cheap. But these two were about five years old, and hopefully would last a while.

His wagon also had wider, thicker wheels and axles than most. Again, this was because of the weight he carried.

Wellington—who preferred to be called C.W.—was in his late thirties and figured this was his last shot to make a name for himself. He had tried staying in one place and doing it, but that never worked. So he decided to travel and try to establish himself that way. The only thing he knew he wouldn't be able to do was run. If he was ever chased by outlaws or Indians, they'd catch him in a minute. His wagon and Clydesdales were not built for speed.

He was heading south through Montana Territory, thinking that maybe Idaho was the place for him to make his start. Or perhaps Wyoming Territory.

He also wondered if he should have given his horses names?

***

Clint Adams was riding through Wyoming Territory, enjoying the end of two weeks on the trail without running into trouble, or even seeing anybody. He had stuffed his saddlebags, and a canvas sack, with enough supplies to keep him from having to stop in a town. He wasn't missing human contact, at all. But this far in, it was about time for him to reoutfit himself if he wanted to stay on the trail.

He came to a town he'd never been to before, called Makerville, in Wyoming. The sign he had seen indicated it had a small population, which appealed to him. All he needed was a mercantile store, which most towns had, no matter their size. If there was also a saloon, he would stop for only one beer, and then ride on out.

That was the plan.

***

Caleb Wellington drove his wagon into Makerville. It was a small town and he probably wouldn't find any business there, but he felt as if he could use a cold beer before continuing his search for a place to ply his trade.

He drove his wagon past several abandoned buildings and the mercantile. Then, when he saw the saloon, he reined in the two Clydesdales and applied the brake.

There were two men standing out in front of the saloon, staring at him.

"What the hell is that?" one of them asked.

C.W. climbed down and faced the men. They towered over him, as he was only five and a half feet tall.

"It's my business," he said.

"It looks like a goddamned railroad car," the man told him.

"And what are those?" the other man asked, pointing.

"Those are my horses."

"Those are horses?" the first man asked. "What the hell kind?"

"They're Clydesdales. Bred to pull wagons."

"They're ugly as sin," the second man said. "You gotta get 'em outta our town."

"I'm not going to be here long," C.W. said. "I just want a beer."

He walked past them and entered the saloon.

"I don't think he understood," the first man said.

"Maybe we better go in and tell 'im again," the other man said.

They turned and went through the batwing doors to-gether.

**

Clint Adams rode into town, spotted the mercantile right away, but then he saw the saloon and decided on a beer first. He rode Eclipse over to it and around the huge wagon that was parked out front. He dismounted, dropped Eclipse's reins to the ground, then took a moment to examine the two Clydesdales hitched to the wagon. They were impressive beasts. It was quite a rig.

He went into the saloon.

Chapter Two

Clint stopped just inside the doors. There were only a few men present, but he thought he was able to pick out the one attached to the wagon. The little man was the only one who looked like a drummer, with a dark suit and a bowler hat.

There were two other men standing at the end of the bar near the window, who looked like brothers. The drummer seemed to be the object of their angry glares. He was standing in the center of the bar, sipping a beer. Clint walked to the far end and waved to the bartender.

"Beer," he said.

"Sure."

The bartender put a mug in front of him, then leaned back and waited to see what was going to happen. Ever since the Tolan Brothers had walked in, he knew they had something against the little guy.

***

Eddie and Frank Tolan stood at the bar, staring at the small man with the big wagon and ugly horses.

"Hey, you," Eddie said.

The little man didn't look at them.

"Hey," Frank yelled, "my brother's talkin' to you."

Now the smaller man looked over at them.

"I'm just trying to enjoy my beer, and then I'll get out of your town."

"We think we should do somethin' to clean up our town, now," Frank, the older brother, said.

"Like shoot those horses," Eddie said. He was in his twenties, about ten years younger than his brother.

"What?" the small man asked. "Why would you do that?"

"We told you," Frank said. "They're ugly."

The little man turned to face them.

"Sirs," he said, "that doesn't make sense. You want me to leave your town, but if you shoot my horses, I won't be able to."

"Sure you will," Eddie said. "You can walk."

"Not with my wagon."

"Well, then," Frank said, "you'd have to leave the wagon here."

"Oh, I can't do that," the man said. "It's my livelihood. I wouldn't be able to make a living without it."

"Well then, you're just gonna have to find another way to make a livin' other than sellin' fire water, or some phony medicine," Frank Tolan said.

"I don't deal in medicines—"

"Never mind," Eddie Tolan said. "Time for you to go, Mister."

"Wellington," the little man said, "my name is Caleb Wellington."

"Yeah, we'll put that on your tombstone," Frank Tolan said.

***

Clint knew he should've stayed on the trail away from people. If he could, he'd close his eyes, finish his beer, and let the two brothers do whatever they wanted to the little man. But he couldn't do that. He waved the bartender over.

"Who are those two?" he asked.

"The Tolan brothers," the bartender said, "Frank and Eddie."

"Which is which?"

"The younger one is Eddie."

"What will they do to him?" Clint asked.

"If he doesn't leave?" the barman asked. "They'll kill 'im."

"Great."

"You want another one?"

"No," Clint said. He finished the one he had and slammed the mug down hard on the bar. The sound reverberated throughout the room. The Tolans and Wellington all looked.

"Time for you fellows to leave," Clint said.

"What?" Frank asked.

"You talkin' to us?" Eddie asked.

"Yes," Clint said, "I'm talking to both of you."

"This ain't none of your business, friend," Frank said. "Butt out."

"Yeah," Eddie chimed in.

"You're making it my business," Clint said.

"How're we doin' that, huh?" Frank asked, thrusting his chin out.

"Yeah, how?" Eddie demanded. He also did the chin thrust, and Clint assumed it was a family trait.

"Because two-against-one is never fair," Clint said.

"Yeah?" Frank asked. "How would you like it if it was us two against you?"

"Well, that wouldn't be fair either," Clint said. "You two would be outmatched."

"Is that a fact?" Eddie asked.

The two Tolans stepped away from the bar and let their hands dangle down by their holsters.

"Let's find out," Frank said.

Chapter Three

"Now gents, just wait a second," Wellington said. "You fellas can't fight over me."

"Shut up!" Frank Tolan shouted. "You're next after we take care of this guy."

"Relax, Mr. Wellington," Clint said. "This isn't going to take long."

"You're crazy, Mister," Frank Tolan said. "We own this town."

"You call this a town?" Clint asked. "It's a puddle."

"Yeah, maybe," Eddie said, "but it's our puddle. You walk outta here, and nothin' will happen to you."

"And then we'll take care of you," Frank said, pointing at Wellington.

"I'm not going anywhere," Clint said.

"You're willin' to face the two of us?" Frank Tolan asked.

"Facing women is nothing new to me," Clint said.

"Huh?" Eddie said.

He and Frank exchanged a look.

"Who the hell are you?" Frank asked.

"The name's Clint Adams," Clint said. "Are you two ready?"

"I am," Eddie said.

"Wait!" his older brother said. "Adams. I know that name." He looked at Clint. "You're the Gunsmith?"

"That's right."

"What the hell—" Eddie snapped.

"Back off, Eddie!" Frank said. "We ain't throwin' down on the Gunsmith. He'll kill us both without blinkin' an eye."

"How do we know he's the Gunsmith?" Eddie asked. "He could just be sayin' that."

"Bartender," Clint said, "toss a shot glass into the air."

The bartender rushed to obey, picked up and tossed it across the room in a high arch. Clint drew and fired. The glass shattered.

"Damn!" Frank said.

"Aw, that coulda been luck, Frank," Eddie said. "Let 'im do three of 'em."

"Can you do one?" Frank asked his brother. "Shit, not even by accident." He looked at Clint. "We're leavin', Adams. No hard feelin's."

"None at all," Clint said.

Frank Tolan shoved his brother through the batwing doors while the younger man was still complaining.

"That was impressive," Wellington said.

"Thanks," Clint said, ejecting the spent shell and replacing it with a live one, before holstering his gun. "I don't usually like to do trick shooting."

"What if you had missed?" Wellington asked.

Clint stared at him and said, "I don't understand the question."

Wellington laughed.

"How about letting me buy you a drink?" he asked.

***

Sometime later Clint woke slowly, finding himself in the dark.

"What the—" he said, reaching up and encountering a ceiling. Where the hell am I, he thought?

He felt around, found that he was in an enclosed space. It felt like a wooden box, and then it struck him. He was inside a coffin.

Momentarily panicked, he began to struggle, trying to break out by punching and kicking, but the box seemed to be very solidly built.

Exhausted, he stopped and took the time to think back, to try and trace the activity that might have led to this . . .

***

He remembered agreeing to let Wellington buy him a beer. They took their mugs and sat at a table.

"Caleb Wellington," the little man said, sticking out his hand. "Just call me C.W."

"Clint Adams." They shook hands. "Just call me Clint."

"Well, Clint, I owe you my thanks, perhaps even my life," C.W. said. "But could you have shot both those men?"

"I could've, yes," Clint said.

"Amazing," C.W. said. "How wonderful to be that confident."

"You seemed pretty confident dealing with them," Clint said. "I mean, you didn't seem to be panicking."

"Perhaps I was being foolish," Wellington said, "but I didn't think they'd actually shoot me because they didn't like the way my horses and wagon looked."

"Normally, I'd agree," Clint said. "But you have to understand when you're dealing with idiots."

"I suppose I'll have to learn that if I intend to stay in the West and ply my trade."

"That's an impressive rig you have out there," Clint said. "And a fine looking team. Clydesdales, aren't they?"

"You know your horse flesh," C.W. said.

"Why did you choose them?" Clint asked.

"Stamina," C.W. said, "and strength. That's what I needed for my profession."

"And your profession is . . . a drummer?" Clint asked. "What do you sell?"

"I'm not a drummer," C.W. said, "but I am selling something."

"And what would that be?" Clint asked.

"A final resting place," C.W. said. "You see, I'm a mortician."

"Mortician?" Clint asked. "You mean . . . an undertaker?"

"Exactly," C.W. said. "I'm a traveling undertaker."

Chapter Four

After resting for a short time, Clint lit a match and examined the interior of the box he was in. It was smooth, with not the slightest sign of wear. Briefly, he considered setting the box on fire, but he probably would have burned to death before being able to get out, so he extinguished the flame.

Again, he tried to break free before going back to piecing together the events that led to his being inside a coffin . . .

***

"A traveling undertaker?" he'd asked. "I've never heard of that."

"Neither had I when I came up with the idea," Wellington admitted.

"How did it occur to you?"

"Easily, actually," Wellington said. "I have been unable, on several occasions, to set up a business in a town. It seems many people are satisfied with burying their dead themselves, without paying for my services."

"I've seen many undertakers in many towns doing a fine business."

"Yes, but I believe they were probably locals, accepted by the townspeople. I came here from England to try and set myself up in business, but I've not been very welcomed."

"England? I don't hear much of an accent."

"In England there are various types of accents," Wellington said. "When I arrived here in the East, it appeared I was able to blend in somewhat, especially in places like Boston and New York."

"Why not set up shop there, then?" Clint asked.

"I briefly considered Boston or New York, but quickly learned I would not be welcomed. There were already many undertakers in place and apparently no room for me. So eventually I went back to my original plan and came West. But being unable to set myself up in business anywhere I tried—St. Louis, Kansas City, Wichita—I worked my way west and continued to fail. When I was run out of Helena, in Montana Territory, I decided perhaps traveling might be the answer."

"But that rig—"

"It had to be large enough and strong enough for me to carry my tools and, of course, some samples of my work."

"Coffins?"

"Indeed," C.W. said. "You know, here's a thought. How would you like to invest?"

"Invest?"

"Yes, in me, and my products and services. Perhaps even be a partner. I believe I need someone who's familiar with the West."

"I don't think I've ever seen myself as an undertaker, C.W.," Clint said, rejecting the idea.

"I'd be the undertaker," C.W. said, "you're simply my . . . agent. Perhaps you could even ride ahead and pave the way for—"

"A funeral drummer?" Clint said, cutting him off. "I don't think so."

"Perhaps if you came outside and I could show you my wares, you'd change your mind," C.W. suggested.

"I don't think so," Clint said, again. "I'll be moving along right after I finish this beer."

"Then let me buy you another," Wellington said, "just to send you on your way."

"I think I've had—"

"Come, come," Wellington said, standing, "you saved my life. One more!" He turned and hurried to the bar before Clint could say no . . .

***

He remembered the little undertaker coming back to the table with two more beers, then toasting Clint's health. They drank down their beers . . . but Clint couldn't remember finishing his.

Now, as he ran his hands over the wood above him again, he realized his month was feeling very dry, and there was an odd taste on his tongue.

Damn it to hell!

That little sonofabitch had drugged him!

That last beer had been meant to incapacitate him. But how had the small man managed to get him to his rig and into a coffin? And where was Eclipse?

Clint moved his hands down his body to his holster—only it wasn't there. The gun and holster had been removed, probably so he wouldn't be able to shoot his way out of the box.

So was he being buried alive, or was Caleb Wellington just using this method to show off the quality of his wares?

With a new eye Clint once again lit a match and examined the interior of the box. The work was very good, the box very solid. Wellington knew his stuff, apparently. He tried kicking but didn't have enough room to do it effectively. The box was a good fit for him.

He intended to break the man's jaw when he got out.

Chapter Five

Clint became aware of a rocking movement, so he assumed he was in the back of Wellington's rig. He stopped struggling, as he seemed to have enough air. He figured the little man would let him out eventually, thinking he'd made his point. If he'd wanted him dead, he would have put him in this coffin already dead.

The only problem he seemed to be having was the heat. It had to be hot inside the wagon, and even hotter in this box. He was sweating profusely, so if Wellington didn't let him out soon, he might dissolve into a puddle—or drown inside the box.

But that wasn't actually the only problem he was having. He felt a total fool for allowing this to happen. He had let the British undertaker get the best of him, and for that he wasn't about to soon forgive himself. It seemed the older he was getting, the dumber he was becoming. If that continued, it would soon be the death of the Gunsmith.

Eventually, the rocking stopped and he heard what sounded like somebody moving around. A door opened, and then closed and, finally, somebody was right outside the box.

And then the lid was removed. There was light, and cooler air, but also room for him to sit up, which he did, with some difficulty.

"Here you go," Wellington said, handing him a canteen.

"Anymore drugs in this?" Clint asked, dryly.

"No, no just water," C.W. assured him.

He drank some down, and then more, trying to wash away the taste of whatever the undertaker had given him.

"Now let me have my gun back," he said, "so I can shoot you."

"Now, now," Wellington said, "take it easy. I was just trying to make a point."

"By putting me in a coffin?" Clint demanded. "Are you crazy, man?"

"I anticipated that you would be upset, at first," Wellington said.

"Upset?"

"It's late," Wellington said. "Why don't we go outside so you can get some fresh air. We'll camp and I'll build a fire and get some food cooked. While we eat we can talk, and then if you want to kill me, I won't be able to stop you."

"Just let me the hell out of here," Clint said, climbing out of the box.

Wellington moved to the rear of the wagon and opened the doors. Clint scurried outside, stood up straight, took deep breaths and stretched his back. It was a cool night for spring, but the inside of the wagon and box had been stifling.

"I'll build a fire," Wellington said.

Clint saw that the undertaker had tied Eclipse's reins to the back of the wagon. Clint untied the Darley Arabian and stroked his neck.

"A crazy man, that's what he is, boy," he said. "A crazy man."

***

Wellington prepared some bacon-and-beans and coffee.

"One of the things I liked about this kind of traveling through the West is the simplicity of the trail food," he commented.

They were sitting around the fire. Clint had his gun-belt back on. He'd had to quell the desire to shoot the little man, but Wellington's attitude seemed to extinguish the urge.

"You drugged me and, I assume, dragged me outside and put me in that box, all to prove a point," Clint said.

"The bartender helped me, after I assured him that you simply couldn't hold your liquor. He helped me put you in the back of my wagon. I had to get you into the coffin myself."

"And you don't feel any guilt about it?" Clint asked.

"Guilt? It's not as if I buried you alive to prove my point. It was only a matter of hours."

"I could've suffocated in there."

"Not in a few hours," C.W. said. "Come now, tell me what you think of my work."

Clint couldn't believe he was actually about to compliment the man.

"The craftsmanship is excellent," he admitted.

"In the morning I will show you the interior of my wagon," Wellington said. "You didn't take a good look at that while we were in there."

"No," Clint said, "I was in kind of a hurry to get out."

Wellington picked up the pan from the fire.

"There's a bit more here."

Clint held out his plate and Wellington scraped the pan clean.

"I can see you're still very upset by what I did," Wellington said, "so I am going to apologize."

"It was a more than a little crazy, Wellington," Clint pointed out.

"C.W., please," Wellington said. "I admit it was a somewhat desperate move, Clint, but I am feeling somewhat desperate, these days."

"Look," Clint said, "at this point now, I plan to sleep on whether or not I should shoot you or break your jaw in the morning."

"Well," Wellington said, "failing either one of those, perhaps you'll decide to actually invest in what I'm doing, instead."

"I really don't think that's going to be an option, C.W.," Clint said.

Chapter Six

In the morning Clint woke to the smell of bacon and coffee. C.W. was crouched by the fire as Clint approached. The undertaker looked at him over his shoulder.

"I was just about to wake you," he said. "How do you like burned bacon?"

"Crunchy and burned is fine," Clint said.

"Good, because that's the way it's coming out." He turned and held out a cup. "Coffee?"

"Thanks," Clint said, taking it.

He walked around and crouched down on the other side of the fire.

"That horse of yours," C.W. said. "I thought mine were impressive, but that one. What breed is it?"

"He's a Darley Arabian," Clint said. "His name's Eclipse."

"You refer to the horse as he?"

"He *is* a male," Clint pointed out.

"Well, yes, but . . . it's an animal."

"Horses have personalities," Clint said. "The one I had before this was a gelding named Duke. We were partners for a long time. Now Eclipse and I have been partners for a long time. I wouldn't refer to my partner as 'it'."

"I understand."

"What do you call your Clydesdales?" Clint asked.

"They don't have names," C.W. said. "It's odd, but only recently I've wondered if I should have named them. People name their pets, right? Dogs? Cats?"

"These aren't pets," Clint said, "these are partners. The grey one's a female, and the other one's a male. What are they, about five?"

"Exactly."

"They have personalities," Clint said. "How long have you had them?"

"A few months."

"Then they should've shown you by now. Come on, what are their names? Start with the grey one."

"Well . . . she is stubborn, opinionated, and wants to go her own way."

"Well, if she was a he I'd call him Custer," Clint said.

"How about . . . Victoria?" C.W. asked.

"Are you sure your Queen would go for that?" Clint asked.

"She will never know," C.W. said.

"All right, now the male," Clint said. "Maybe you can stick with the theme you started with Victoria."

"He is smart, and crafty," C.W. said. "I am going to call him . . . Dickens."

"There you go," Clint said, raising his mug. "Here's to Victoria and Dickens."

They drank, and then C.W. portioned out the burned bacon.

***

Clint rode alongside C.W.'s wagon after they broke camp.

"So what are your plans?" Clint asked. "Just to ride from town to town, waiting for someone to die so you can sell their family your services?"

"Pretty much, yes," C.W. said, with a shrug. "Of course, it would be ideal for some famous outlaw to die so I could put my wares on display for people to see. I have heard that has been done here in the West."

"It has," Clint said, "but it's in real bad taste."

"So then you wouldn't invest if I did something like that?" the Brit asked.

"Not a chance."

"So then you're saying there *is* a chance you will invest," C.W. said.

"I'm not saying that, either," Clint said. "I'm just saying there's definitely no chance in hell if you're going to put dead men on display."

"I wouldn't actually be putting the men on display, but my coffins—all right, I get your point."

"Where are you headed now?"

"I was thinking about Wyoming."

"I'm going that way, too," Clint admitted.

"Good, then we can ride together, and I can work on you further."

"C.W.—"

"Let me tell you what kind of wood I use to construct my boxes . . ."

***

C.W. talked non-stop for miles, and, if Clint hadn't committed himself to Wyoming, he might have jerked on Eclipse's rein and just lit out. But he stuck with it, and the man finally wore down.

When Clint did rein in, C.W. also stopped.

"What is it?" he asked.

"We're here."

"Where?"

"Wyoming Territory," Clint said. "Time to part company."

"Must we?" C.W. asked. "What if I am attacked again?"

"Do you know what I think will help?" Clint said. "Paint something on the side of your wagon."

"Like what? Undertaker? How would that make things better?" C.W. asked.

"Well, for one thing people won't wonder what you are," Clint said. "And how about 'Traveling Undertaker.' That would certainly make people curious."

"Is that what I want?" C.W. asked. "For people to be curious?"

"A different kind of curious," Clint added. "At least they won't think you're selling some kind of mystic water or medicine."

"You see," C.W. said, "this is why I need your help. I'm new to the West, and I do not know how to behave."

"How long have you been out here?"

"I took a train from New York a couple of months ago. I ended up in Denver, where I bought the team and had the wagon built. I've been on the trail less than two weeks."

"From Denver?"

"Helena, Montana."

"How did you get there?"

"I was looking for a special wagon and heard one was for sale there."

"You've gone through a lot of trouble putting this rig together."

"Yes, I have," C.W. said. "I've tried many towns in Montana, large and small, but to no avail. So now I think I'll try Wyoming. I thought about Idaho Territory, but decided on Wyoming."

"I think you'll do a lot better with something painted on the side of your wagon," Clint said. "Let people know what you're about, and what you do."

"All right," C.W. said. "I'll stop at the next town and buy some paint. Can you ride with me until we get there? Give me some more advice?"

Clint thought about it. His only intention had been to ride through Wyoming. He wasn't going anywhere in particular. And if he rode with C.W., but did the talking, then the man wouldn't be chattering on and on.

"All right, I'll tell you what," Clint said. "I'll ride along, just to the next town. But you listen all the way, you don't talk."

"What if I have a question?"

"You can ask questions, my friend, but that's it," Clint said. "Jesus, has anyone ever told you that you talk too much, and too fast?"

"Many people, I'm afraid," C.W. said. "But I will do my best."

Chapter Seven

The first town they came to in Wyoming was called Southfork, although Clint couldn't see why. There was no fork in the road leading in.

It was a fair-sized place with a few saloons, a hotel, and a decent looking mercantile where they thought C.W. could get the paint he needed.

"Should I buy one brush or two?" C.W. asked, as they stopped in front.

"One. I said I'd ride with you and give you advice. I didn't say I'd paint."

"Just checking," C.W. said.

Clint waited outside while the Brit went in. As people walked past, they paused or stopped to look at the wagon and eye the Clydesdale team. Clint nodded at the men and touched the brim of his hat to the ladies.

When C.W. came out, he was carrying a can of white paint and a sack that seemed to hang heavy with items.

"What's in there?" Clint asked.

"I got a brush, but while I was there I thought I would get some canned peaches, beans and beef jerky."

Clint nodded. He hadn't decided just how long he would ride with C.W., but peaches, beans and jerky would make it easier.

C.W. stowed his purchases in the back of his wagon, then walked around to the front and climbed aboard.

"I guess we should find someplace I can do the painting," he said.

"Outside of town would work," Clint said. "And we can camp."

"Fine with me," C.W. said.

They continued on through town and out the other side, traveling until they found a likely clearing with room to camp and to work on the wagon.

"I'll make camp while you get started," Clint said. "By the time you get the first line done, coffee should be ready."

C.W. opened his paint can and stirred. Paint cans had only been in existence for about ten years. Before cans, unused paint would have to be discarded, but now it could be saved and used later.

"So you suggest 'Traveling Undertaker,'" C.W. said.

"Yes," Clint said. "It will catch people's curiosity."

Clint set about building a fire and getting the coffee going while C.W. got a small ladder out of the back of his wagon and proceeded with the painting. By the time he was done with the word "TRAVELING" Clint went over and handed him a cup of coffee.

"How does it look?" he asked.

He stepped down from the ladder and they both moved back a few steps. He had painted the word in large, block letters that could be seen very clearly.

"Looks good so far," Clint said. "I'll get some beans started."

"And open a can of peaches," C.W. requested. "I have a taste for them."

"Comin' up," Clint promised.

C.W. got back up onto the ladder and painted the word "UNDERTAKER." Then beneath that, in smaller letters, he painted "Caleb Wellington."

They still had plenty of light, so he was able to sit at the fire with Clint and eat, before going back to the wagon and painting the other side.

They wolfed down the beans, shared the can of peaches—although Clint made sure C.W. got most of them—and then the Brit went back to work while Clint cleaned up and made another pot of coffee.

As dusk fell C.W. finished the job, sealed the paint can and put it and the ladder in the wagon. He then used some water from a barrel that was affixed to the wagon and washed the brush, leaving it out to dry.

"All right, then," he said, accepting another cup of coffee from Clint, "tomorrow we will see if this makes a difference."

"It might take more than a day or two, C.W.," Clint pointed out.

"Even that will be all right," C.W. said. "I just need to receive some kind of attention and encouragement."

Clint had to wonder if that would ever happen? Undertaker didn't seem to him the kind of business you could do while traveling. He just felt that C.W. was in for some more disappointment.

Chapter Eight

In the morning, they checked the wagon to see if the paint had dried without running.

"You did a good job," Clint said.

"I have artistic tendencies," C.W. bragged. "I once thought I would be an artist, before I decided to be an undertaker."

"That seems to be two very different directions your life could've taken," Clint observed.

"Not really," C.W. said. "I use my art in my work now."

"I can't comment on that," Clint said, "since I haven't seen your work, yet. Let's get Victoria and Dickens cinched up and ready to go."

"I can do that," C.W. said. "You might as well saddle Eclipse. And break camp."

"Right."

Clint doused the fire, then saddled Eclipse and stowed their supplies, some in his saddlebags, some in the rear of the wagon. By the time he was done, the two Clydesdales were ready to go.

"Do you have any idea what the next town is?" C.W. asked.

"We're not near Cody yet, but if we keep traveling east, we'll get there—Sheridan, too, eventually. But before that you might want to head south."

"Back toward Denver?"

Clint nodded.

"They might understand what you're doing there, more than anywhere else. You could try Colorado, Nebraska . . ."

"I think I should give Wyoming a chance, don't you?" C.W. asked. "But I did ask for your advice."

"This is not advice," Clint said. "Just a suggestion."

"Let's see what happens when we get to Cody," C.W. said. "That's a large place, isn't it?"

"It is."

"Good. Then let's proceed."

Clint nodded, and mounted up.

***

Before they came to Cody, they reached a town called Venture. It was larger than Southfork had been, with hotels and saloons, but there weren't many people on the street.

"A town this large," C.W. said, as they rode in, "somebody must have died recently."

34

"I don't think that's something you want to ask," Clint said. "Let's just see if anyone reacts to what you've written on the side of your wagon."

"I think we should register at one of these hotels and leave the wagon out front for people to see," C.W. said. "We can get a hot meal, spend the night in a hotel bed, and see what the morning brings."

"If that's what you want to do," Clint said. "When we check in, though, just don't ask the hotel clerk if anyone died recently."

"If you insist," C.W. said.

They stopped the wagon in front of the One Tree Hotel, and Clint dismounted. People on the street paused to read what was written on the side of C.W.'s wagon, then walked off, frowning.

At the front desk, they each got a room and then, as Clint was walking to the stairs with his saddlebags and rifle, he heard C.W. ask the clerk. Does this town have an undertaker?"

He didn't hear the answer.

When he got to his room, he dropped off his gear, then turned and left immediately. He had to get Eclipse to a livery stable.

Whatever the clerk's answer to the question had been, it held C.W. up long enough so that they passed in the hall.

"Was that question necessary?" Clint asked.

"I didn't ask if anyone died," C.W. argued.

"What did he say?"

"They have an undertaker who has, apparently, been here for a long time."

"Look," Clint said, "if we're going to stay overnight, you can't leave the wagon out front."

"Why not?"

"The horses need to be boarded, brushed and fed," Clint said. "They can't stand on the street all night."

"Yes, yes," C.W said, "you're right about that. But perhaps we can leave the wagon outside the livery stable."

"Let's go and find out."

C.W. didn't have any gear to drop in his room, so he turned and followed Clint back down the stairs.

When they got out to the front of the hotel, they saw a group of men gathered by C.W.'s wagon. They all turned and looked at Clint and C.W. The man in front was wearing a badge.

"This your wagon?" he asked.

"It's mine," C.W. said. "Why?"

"What's that mean, on the side there? 'Traveling Undertaker.'?"

"Just what it says," C.W. told him. "I travel, and I perform undertaker services."

"That means you do funerals?" the lawman asked.

"Yes."

"And you do coffins?"

"I do."

"And you bury people?"

"Yes."

The sheriff turned and exchanged some glances with the other men. Clint counted at least a dozen.

Clint wondered what this was leading to?

Chapter Nine

"Well," the sheriff said, "we already got an undertaker."

"I heard that from the desk clerk," C.W. said.

"So I guess you better leave town," the lawman said.

"Why?" Clint asked.

The lawman looked him over.

"You with him?"

"We rode in together."

"Then I guess you better get on your horse and leave town, too."

"You haven't answered my question," Clint said. "Why?"

"Like I said," the sheriff answered, "we already got an undertaker."

"So," Clint said, "nobody has to use Mr. Wellington's services if they don't want to. We just got rooms at this hotel. I don't see why we should leave."

Now the sheriff gave Clint all of his attention. He was a tall man in his early fifties, wearing a badge that appeared to be as worn as the shirt it was pinned to. The shirt was faded blue, with frayed cuffs and collar.

"I can see his name on the side of the wagon," the lawman said. "What's your name?"

"Clint Adams."

A wave of murmurs went through the men who were standing behind the sheriff. Some of them seemed prepared to turn and walk away.

"The Gunsmith?" the sheriff asked.

"That's right."

"How do I know you're tellin' the truth?"

"You don't," Clint said, "but who would lie about a thing like that, and paint a target on his back?"

"You got a point," the lawman said.

"About the lie, or about us staying in town?"

The lawman chewed his mustache for a moment, then said, "Both, I guess."

"Then we'll stay," Clint said, "and mind our own business."

"Stay for how long?" the sheriff asked.

"We've got no business here," Clint said, "so we'll just get a meal and a good night's sleep, and be on our way by morning. That suit you, Sheriff?"

"It suits me just fine, Mr. Adams," the sheriff said. He turned. "Come on boys, move along. Nothin' to see here."

Some of the men shuffled away, some walked quickly. The sheriff turned back to Clint and C.W.

"You gents have a nice day," he said, then turned and walked away.

"That was fascinating," C.W. said. "I believe they were prepared to run us out of town, until you said your name."

"I think you're right," Clint said. "Come on, C.W., let's get these horses over to the livery stable."

***

The hostler at the stable was very pleased to take Eclipse into his barn, and also seemed fascinated by C.W.'s Clydesdales.

"I heard of this breed, but I ain't never seen 'em," he said. "They look mighty strong."

"That's why I bought them," C.W. said.

"Well, gents, I'll take good care of all three of these animals. How long you gonna be stayin'?"

"Probably overnight," Clint said.

"Do you mind if I leave my wagon out front?" C.W. asked.

"Don't make no never mind to me, friend, but I gotta tell ya, we already got us an undertaker in town."

"So we've heard," C.W. said.

"I gotta warn ya," the man went on, "he's the sheriff's brother, so you might be hearin' from Sheriff Sullivan."

"We already did," Clint said. "We've come to an understanding."

"Really?" the man said. "That surprises me."

"What can I say?" Clint asked. "I'm convincing."

As they left, C.W. asked, "Why didn't you tell him your name?"

"It's bad enough it's in the hotel register, and the sheriff and those men know it," Clint said. "I don't want to spread it around any further."

***

Once the horses were lodged, Clint suggested they get something to eat. C.W. was all for that idea.

"As much as I like bacon and beans, I am ready for a good meal."

They had passed a likely looking café on the way to the livery, so Clint pointed to it on the way back.

"Let's go in there."

They entered, found it half full, so there were plenty of tables. Clint was able to choose one he wanted, near the back.

They received some curious looks from the few customers as they were shown to their table.

Chapter Ten

"The sheriff is the undertaker's brother," C.W. said. "Do you think that was the only reason he was trying to make us leave town?"

"Who knows?" Clint said. "What matters is that he backed off."

The waiter brought them both the steak suppers they had ordered.

"I truly love the way you cook steak out here," C.W. said.

"I was in England once," Clint said, "years ago."

"Really? Why?"

"For a gun show," Clint said. "I have to say, I didn't like the food."

"I don't blame you," C.W. said, chewing avidly. "What should we do after we eat? A saloon?"

"Not a good idea," Clint said. "I think we should just go to our rooms."

"But it's so early."

"C.W., I think the sooner you get to Cody the better it'll be for your business."

"And will you see that I get there safely?"

"I will," Clint said. "But from that point on, you're going to be on your own, and so am I."

"I understand."

"So let's just eat and then get back to the hotel," Clint said.

"Are you expecting trouble?"

"I'm always expecting trouble," Clint said.

***

Clint and C.W. walked back to their hotel and went to their rooms. There Clint removed his boots and gun. The bed didn't have a headboard of any kind, so he set the holster down on the night table next to it.

He took the book he was currently reading from his saddlebag. It was Jonathan Swift's 1726 novel *Gulliver's Travels*. He hadn't started it yet but had been looking forward to reading it. Now he was going to have plenty of time to get into it.

***

Down the hall Caleb Wellington was feeling claustrophobic. Even more than when he was in the back of his wagon. He needed to get out, get some air, and have a beer. Clint had suggested they stay in, but he decided to go out, find a saloon and have just one beer.

Or two.

***

Clint started reading his book, but a question popped into his head that he thought an Englishman could answer. He put his boots back on and walked down the hall to C.W.'s room. He knocked three times before he decided C.W. wasn't asleep. He went back to his room, strapped on his gun and went down to the lobby.

At the desk he said, "I need a key to my friend's room. He may be in trouble."

"I don't think so," the desk clerk said.

"Why not?"

"Because he ain't in his room," the clerk said. "He went out."

"When?"

"About twenty minutes ago."

"Do you know where he went?"

"Well . . . he asked me where the closest saloon was."

"All right," Clint said, "now tell me."

***

C.W. found the Five Card Saloon right where the desk clerk said it would be. It was pretty popular, judging from the amount of people he could see inside as he looked over the batwing doors. He stepped through, stopped a moment to look around. There were gaming tables, and girls. But what he was interested in was the bar.

He walked over to it, waved down the bartender.

"Beer, please."

"Yup."

"Hey," somebody called out, "ain't you that undertaker?"

C.W. turned his head to the right, saw a man staring at him.

"Yeah," another man standing next to the first one said, "that's him, that little guy with the big wagon and the weird horses."

"Where's your buddy?" the first man asked. "The Gunsmith? Ain't he gonna be worried about you?"

"I just came in for a beer," C.W. said. "Not for any trouble."

The first man snapped his fingers.

"The Traveling Undertaker, that's who he is," he said.

"You know," the second man said, "we got an undertaker in town."

"So I've been told repeatedly."

"Then what are ya doin' here?" one of them asked. Even as Caleb looked at them, he couldn't tell them apart, didn't know which one had spoken.

"I am just having a beer," he said. "Please leave me alone."

"Whoa," one said, "did you hear him? He's so polite, ain't he?"

"'Please leave me alone,'" the other one repeated, and they both laughed.

One of the saloon girls saw what was going on, and decided to step in.

***

Clint followed the desk clerk's simple directions to the Five Card Saloon. When he got to the front, he heard the laughter from inside and knew the derisive quality of it when he heard it.

He just hoped he wasn't walking into the saloon too late . . .

Chapter Eleven

As Clint entered the crowded saloon, he had no trouble picking out Caleb Wellington. There was a small crowd of men at the bar, and that was where the laughter he had identified was coming from.

There was also a pretty brunette saloon girl standing there, saying, "Why don't you fellas leave him alone? He's just trying to have a beer?"

One of the men said, "Mind your own business, bitch."

"That's no way to talk to a lady," C.W. said.

At that point Clint reached the group.

"Excuse me," he said, pushing his way past the men until he was standing next to C.W. and the girl.

"Clint," C.W. said. "I'm sorry, I just needed a beer, and these men—this nice young lady—"

"Hey, it's the other one," a man said. "That's his friend."

"What'd he say his name was?" another asked.

"I don't know, I didn't hear it," the man said. "He told the sheriff, and the sheriff didn't tell us. He just backed off."

"Wait a minute, wait a minute," a third man said. "I heard . . . he said he was the Gunsmith."

It suddenly got quiet as the men surrounding them fell silent and stared.

"The Gunsmith?" Carly, the saloon girl, asked. "Really?"

"No," one of the men said, "what would the Gunsmith be doin' here?"

"Passing through," Clint said, then looked at the bartender. "Beer."

"Sure."

The bartender set a mug in front of him.

"You fellas mind if I drink this?" he asked, picking it up.

"Sure," one said, "All you gotta do is prove you're the Gunsmith."

Clint sipped and then asked, "Why?"

"What?"

"Why do I have to prove it?" Clint asked. "Who are you fellas?"

"We live here," one said. "We're friends of our undertaker."

"And we don't need him here," another said, pointing at C.W.

"We're not staying," Clint said. "We're on our way to Cody."

"You got business there?" a man asked.

Clint recognized three of the men from the group who had greeted them with the sheriff. Some were standing toward the back and hadn't heard his name.

"He might," Clint said. "Right now we just want to finish these beers and go to our hotel."

"Aw, come on, Mr. . . . . Adams," the ringleader said, laughing and looking around at his friends. "Yeah, Clint Adams, the Gunsmith. We want you to prove it."

"Well," Clint said, examining the men. Some had guns, some didn't. "I could kill those of you who are armed. Would that prove it?"

"Jesus," Carly said, backing away.

The spokesman was wearing a gun, and suddenly he backed away.

"Hey, wait," he said, "there ain't no need for that."

"Good," Clint said, "then we can drink and go."

The men all looked at each other, and then those who had guns moved to the front of the crowd, which had grown.

"We just need one small thing to prove who you are," one said.

"You're serious," Clint said.

"Yeah, we're serious, ain't we, boys?" he asked, and the others nodded. By this time the entire saloon was interested.

"Bartender," Clint said. "when I tell you to, throw three shot glasses into the air."

"What?" the man asked.

"It's an old trick," Clint said, "but it works."

"Yeah, okay."

The man picked up three shot glasses.

"Okay," Clint said, "now!"

Chapter Twelve

The shot glasses flew into the air. Clint drew and fired three times and all three glasses shattered. The saloon fell completely silent—and then suddenly they were cheering.

Clint reloaded his gun, holstered it and picked up his beer.

"Jesus," Carly breathed.

"Drink up," he told C.W. "We have to go."

"Right."

They drained their mugs and set them down on the bar.

"Can we go now?" Clint asked the men.

"Oh my God," the man said, "I never saw anythin' like that before."

The batwings opened and the sheriff walked in.

"What the hell is goin' on?" he demanded.

"Sheriff," one of the men said, "we just wanted the Gunsmith to prove who he was."

"That was the three shots I heard?"

"Three shots," the man repeated, "the shot glasses flew out of the air. It was amazing!"

"Can we go?" Clint asked. "We want to get some sleep so we can get an early start."

"Yeah, yeah, go," the sheriff said. "And do me a favor. Stay in your rooms, this time."

"Understood," Clint said.

He and C.W. left the saloon.

***

When they got to the hotel, Clint said to C.W., "You heard the sheriff. Stay in your room this time."

"Can't we stay in one room?" C.W. asked. "Play cards, or something?"

"No," Clint said. "I want to go to sleep, and you should, too."

"But . . . you are going to Cody with me, aren't you?"

"Yes, I told you," Clint said. "But when we get there, we split up."

"I understand," C.W. said. "All right, then. Good night."

"Good night," Clint said, and they went to their own rooms.

***

There was a knock on Clint's door about an hour later. He wasn't asleep, as he was still reading *Gulliver's*

Travels. He grabbed his gun from the night table and walked to the door.

"Who is it?"

"My name is Paul Sullivan," a voice said. "I'm the town undertaker?"

Clint frowned.

"My brother is the sheriff."

Clint opened the door a crack, looked at the tall, thin man standing in the hall.

"You look like him," Clint said.

"I'm the older brother," Sullivan said. "He looks like me, poor bastard."

"What can I do for you?"

"Can I come in?" Sullivan asked. "Rather than talk out here?"

Clint opened the door, looked out into the hall, then said, "Sure, come on in."

Sullivan slipped in past him, and Clint closed the door. When he turned, the undertaker was looking at his gun.

"You're not gonna need that," he said, lifting his jacket. "I'm unarmed."

Clint walked to the night table and put the gun back in the holster.

"What can I do for you, Mr. Sullivan?" Clint asked.

"I saw the wagon," he said. "The one you left outside the livery stable."

"It's not my wagon."

"I know," Sullivan said, "it belongs to somebody named Caleb Wellington, a Traveling Undertaker."

"Exactly."

"I find that concept . . . fascinating," Sullivan said. "I mean . . . I can't imagine how he must do what we do while traveling."

"I haven't asked him, so I don't know," Clint said.

"I'd like to ask him," Sullivan said.

"Then why didn't you go to his room?"

"Well . . . they told me you're the Gunsmith," Sullivan said. "I was advised that I shouldn't do anything that might make you shoot me."

"Like creep down the hallway?"

"Right."

"All right, then," Clint said. "Go down the hall to room seven and see if Mr. Wellington will talk to you."

"Can you take me there? Introduce me?"

"No," Clint said. "C.W. will have to decide on his own if he wants to talk with you."

"Right, right. Of course. I'm sorry I bothered you."

Clint saw the man to the door, then stopped before opening it.

"Do you have some sort of identification on you?" he asked.

"I thought you might ask that." He took out a piece of paper and handed it over. "I am fully licensed to be an undertaker."

"I wasn't aware you needed a license for the job," Clint admitted. He had simply never thought about it, before.

The man took his license back and said, "They don't let just anybody handle dead bodies, you know."

Chapter Thirteen

Caleb Wellington was about to try to go to sleep when there was a knock on his door. He naturally assumed it was Clint Adams, because who else could it have been? When he opened the door and saw a stranger, he stared, curiously.

"Yes," he asked, "can I help you?"

"My name is Paul Sullivan," the man said. "I'm the town undertaker."

"Ah," C.W. said. "I met your brother."

"Yes," Sullivan said, "the sheriff. He's the one who told me where to find you."

"He also told me to leave town," C.W. said.

"He's always been a little impulsive," Sullivan said. "I think before you leave town we should talk. Do you mind if I come in?"

"By all means," C.W. said, stepping back. "Come in."

***

Before Clint could become immersed with the travels of Lemuel Gulliver, there was another knock on his door. He wondered if Sullivan was stopping again, on his way back from C.W.'s room?

"Who is it?" he asked.

"Um, Carly?" a girl's voice said. "I'm the saloon girl from, uh, the saloon? I saw you there earlier?"

Holding his gun, Clint opened the door a crack. The girl looked startled.

"Oh, uh, all right, hi," she said. "I uh, was wondering if we could talk?"

"About what?"

"Well, about what you did," she said. "It was . . . amazing, and exciting!" she said.

"Carly," he said, "you shouldn't be here—"

"Out in the hall," she said, "I know. Could you let me in before somebody sees me?"

He opened the door to let her enter, stuck his head out, looked both ways, then closed it.

"I didn't bring anybody with me," she assured him.

"Just checking," he said.

He studied her a moment. She was wearing a yellow dress he thought was the same one she'd been wearing earlier, at the saloon. The only place she could've been hiding a gun was in her garter, or her cleavage.

"What's wrong?" she asked.

"You mind pulling your skirt up?"

"What?"

"The skirt."

She looked amused.

"How high?"

"Just to the garters."

She used both hands, lifted the skirt inch by inch until her smooth white skin and garter were showing. No gun.

"That's good, thanks."

"Are you looking for a gun?"

"Just being careful," he said.

"I could have a derringer in my cleavage," she said.

"I was thinking the same thing."

"There's one sure way to find out."

She reached up, pulled the dress off each shoulder, and then peeled it down so that her breasts were bare.

"See a gun?" she asked.

"No."

What he did see were small but solid breasts, pale skin, brown nipples that were slightly hard. He walked to his nightstand and set his gun down there.

"What brought you here, Carly?" he asked.

"Excitement," she said. "It's been a while since I've had any excitement, and watching you shoot those glasses . . . that was thrilling."

"Happy to oblige."

"But you're the Gunsmith," she said. "The excitement doesn't stop there."

She stood up, shimmied her dress down to her ankles and then kicked it away. She was now completely and beautifully naked.

"I want more," she said. "More excitement."

"I suppose I can oblige with that, too," he said.

***

Down the hall the door to room seven opened again. Paul Sullivan stepped out, turned and shook hands with Caleb Wellington.

"We'll be seeing each other again," Sullivan said.

"Yes," C.W. said.

Sullivan nodded, began walking toward the stairway. He stopped in front of Clint Adams' door and listened for a moment. It was fairly obvious from the sounds inside, the man was not alone.

Sullivan smiled, and continued on.

Chapter Fourteen

Clint woke in the morning with Carly lying next to him. She was on her tummy, no sheet on her, so he was able to eye her entire body. He ran his eyes from the base of her neck to the cleft between her taut buttocks. Then he leaned over and did the same thing with his finger.

"Mmmm," she moaned.

"Enough excitement?" he asked.

She rolled over, looked down between his legs, then reached out and grasped his semi-hard cock.

"Not quite yet," she said.

She shimmied down between his legs and took him in her mouth. She sucked him avidly, wetly, until he was fully hard, then she climbed up on him and impaled herself on his rigid penis.

"Just a little more," she whispered, and began to slide up and down on him . . .

***

Later that morning, Clint walked down the hall to C.W.'s room and knocked on the door. This time, the door opened right away.

"Ready to go?" he asked.

"I am ready," the traveling undertaker said.

They went downstairs and checked out of their rooms, then stepped outside. C.W. was empty-handed, while Clint held his rifle and saddlebags.

"Let's get some breakfast. There's a place between here and the livery."

"Right."

They started walking and stopped in the small café along the way. They both ordered bacon-and-eggs and coffee.

"Did you talk to Sullivan?" Clint asked.

"Who?"

"The town undertaker, Mr. Sullivan," Clint said. "He came to my room last night, and then said he was going to yours."

"Well," C.W. said, "he didn't come to my door."

"That's odd."

"What did he want from you?" C.W. asked.

"He wanted information about you," Clint said. "I told him if he wanted to know anything, he should talk to you. That's where I thought he was going when he left my room."

"He never got to me," C.W. said. "Why did you talk to him, at all?"

"He showed me his license," Clint said.

"I didn't know one was needed," C.W. said.

"You don't need a license in England?"

"No."

"So you don't have one in America?"

"I don't," C.W. said.

"Well," Clint said, "maybe with what you do and how you work it, you don't."

"And I don't know who to ask," C.W. admitted, "so I will just wait until something happens."

"You mean, until somebody asks."

"Right."

"Well," Clint said, "until then, I'm still wondering about this fellow Sullivan, and what he really wanted."

"Didn't you say he's the sheriff's brother?"

"Supposedly."

"Do you want to stop and ask him?"

"No," Clint said, "I think we should just leave town. I'll watch our back trail."

"Back trail?" C.W. repeated, frowning.

"I'll keep checking to see if we're being followed."

"Oh, I see. You think someone will be after my wagon?" C.W. asked.

"Or after me," Clint said. "I guess we'll find out. Are you finished?"

C.W. put the last piece of bacon into his mouth and said, "Quite."

***

Sheriff Tom Sullivan looked down at the naked girl in his bed. She was a long, lean, blonde whore named Ellie. Her skin was pale, her nipples pink, the hair between her slim thighs golden.

"Are you gonna just look at me?" she asked. "Or are we gonna fuck."

"What does this look like?" he asked, pointing to his jutting penis.

"It looks like you're ready for some action, but you ain't doin' nothin', Sheriff. Here, lemme help ya."

She reached out, grabbed his hard cock, and began to stroke it.

"How's that?" she asked.

"That's just fine, girl," he told her, closing his eyes. And as she cradled his balls with the other hand, he breathed out a long, "Yeeaaaah."

That's when somebody knocked on the door.

"Shit!" he said.

"Leave it."

He pushed her away and said, "Shut up."

He went to the door naked and opened it.

"Jesus," his brother said. "Put somethin' on."

"Whataya want, Paul?"

"They're gone," he said. "Adams and the undertaker, they checked out of the hotel and they're at the livery."

"Then they ain't gone, are they?" the sheriff said. "Make sure they actually ride out of town, and then come to my office. Don't bother me here, again."

"Yeah, yeah," Paul said, "you don't think I wanna see that."

The sheriff slammed the door and returned to the bed.

"All right," he said, reaching for the girl, "gimme what I'm payin' for."

***

They hitched the Clydesdales to the wagon, saddled Eclipse and rode out. Clint kept his eyes alert for anyone following them, but no one seemed to be coming right from town. They could have been ahead of them, though, waiting.

He probably should have gone to the sheriff to find out if he had a brother named Paul Sullivan. He didn't even know if Sullivan was the sheriff's name. But he made the call to get them out of town before something else happened.

The Traveling Undertaker was traveling again.

Chapter Fifteen

"Anybody following us?" C.W. asked.

"No," Clint said, then "not yet."

C.W. climbed down from his wagon as Clint dismounted.

"I can build the fire and start supper this time," C.W. said. "You know, share the chores?"

"All right," Clint said. "I'll see to the horses."

He unhitched the Clydesdales, strung a picket line, attached them, but left Eclipse standing free after unsaddling him.

By the time he got to the fire C.W. handed him a cup of coffee and had a pan of bacon-and-beans going.

"I wish there was something else to have with this," the undertaker said.

"Next time I cook, I can make some pan biscuits to go with it."

"Biscuits? Over a campfire?"

"Skillet biscuits," Clint said. "It can be done."

"I'll look forward to that," C.W. said, passing a plate across the fire to Clint.

While they ate Clint said, "I want to set up watches for tonight."

"Watches?"

"One of us sleeps, the other one keeps watch," Clint said. "Four hours on, four hours off."

"What am I watching for?" C.W. asked.

"Anything," Clint said. "Anything that doesn't seem right, you wake me up."

"How am I supposed to know—"

"Pay attention to Eclipse."

"Your horse?"

"He'll tell you if something's wrong," Clint said.

"And how will it—he knows?"

"It'll be something he hears, sees, smells or just . . . senses. If he acts up at all, wake me up. But I'll take the first watch. I'll wake you in four hours."

"All right."

C.W. bedded down underneath his wagon, rather than inside. Clint put another pot of coffee on the fire, placed his rifle across his knees. He looked over at where Eclipse was standing with the Clydesdales.

So far there had been no indication that anyone was behind them, or ahead of them. But Clint still couldn't ignore the fact that someone had come to his room, identifying himself as the town undertaker, and then disappeared.

Unless he did talk with C.W., and the Brit was lying. But why would that be? He couldn't think of a reason.

***

Clint drank an entire pot of coffee in the first four hours, so he made another one for C.W. before waking him.

"Jesus," C.W. said, rolling out from beneath his wagon. "Was that four hours?"

"It was," Clint said. "Here." He handed C.W. his rifle.

"What am I supposed to do with this?"

"Shoot anything that comes near the camp, or moves."

"All right."

"Just don't shoot me," Clint said, "or the horses."

"I'll try not to."

"And have breakfast ready when you wake me."

"Yessir!"

Clint ignored the tone and settled down to get his four hours.

***

Clint woke on his own to the smell of bacon and coffee. He rolled over and looked at C.W., who was crouched over the fire. The rifle was on the ground next to him. As he stood up and walked to the fire, C.W. grabbed the rifle and turned.

"Easy," Clint said, "remember I told you not to shoot me."

"I know you did," the undertaker said, "and I'm sorry about this."

C.W. fired the rifle. The bullet hit Clint in the right side. Instead of grabbing the wound, or his gun, he could only turn and run, because suddenly, he couldn't use his right arm.

As he ran, he heard another shot from behind him. What he didn't hear was the sound of the bullet flying past him. He just hoped against hope that C.W.—if that was even his name—hadn't shot Eclipse.

He continued to run until his legs started to give out, and then he fell to the ground and rolled down an embankment. He was unconscious before he reached the bottom . . .

***

He woke to find himself still alive. It was a pleasant discovery.

He pushed himself to a seated position and looked around. Obviously, C.W. hadn't found him.

He took a moment, then got to his feet and started to walk back to the campsite. When he got there the wagon was gone.

Chapter Sixteen

He walked to the fire, found the ashes still warm. He was thankful not to find Eclipse lying on the ground. He had been afraid that last shot he'd heard had been meant for the Darley Arabian. But the horse was smart and had probably lit out when he heard the first shot.

Luckily, C.W. had left Clint's saddle, saddlebags, and canteen behind, choosing not to take them with him. The canteen was almost full, and he took several healthy swigs. Then he sat down by the saddle and lifted his shirt to examine the wound. It appeared the bullet had gone in and out. He flexed his right arm, which seemed to be working now. He could have put C.W. down before he fired again, instead of running. He didn't know of a nerve that ran from his arm to his side, but there must have been one, and there had to have been a momentary disconnect.

He took an extra shirt out of his saddlebag, tore it up and tried to fashion a bandage for the wound, one that would at least slow the bleeding, if not stop it. Once that was done, he got to his feet.

The only thing the traveling undertaker had taken with him was Clint's rifle. There was no way Clint could carry the saddle, so he took his saddlebags—putting them over his uninjured left shoulder—and canteen and started walking. He was hoping he'd be able to pick up Eclipse's trail.

Or find help.

***

He found Eclipse's tracks and followed them. They were fresh and the Darley seemed to be walking, not running. Finally, he came over a rise and saw the big horse standing still, as if waiting for him. As he approached, the horse looked back, almost as if to say, it's about time.

"How you doing, boy?" Clint asked. "Better than me, I hope."

He ran his hands over the animal and was relieved to find no wounds.

"I don't know what that damn little Brit had in mind," Clint said to Eclipse, "but luckily he wasn't very good with that rifle."

Clint would have preferred riding from that point on, but without a saddle, he wasn't able to hoist himself up onto Eclipse's back. At least, not without doing some damage to his wound.

"Come on, big fella," he said to Eclipse, "let's keep walking."

***

Clint had been splitting the water between himself and Eclipse—allowing the animal to drink from his hand, as his hat had gotten lost in the scuffle. So he felt lucky to spot a house in the distance as he drank the last of his water. He just hoped the place also had a well.

As he approached with Eclipse close behind him, he heard a woman's voice shout, "Stop right there!"

He stopped and looked at the rifle barrel which was sticking out one of the windows. The house looked old, but well cared for. There was no barn, no corral, and from his vantage point he didn't see a well.

"Whataya want here?" the voice asked.

"I need help," he called back. "I've been shot."

"Are you wanted by the law?"

"No, Ma'am."

"Just stay there."

The rifle barrel withdrew, and the front door opened. A tall, angular woman with long brown hair stepped out, and once again the rifle was pointed at him.

"Yeah," she said, "I can see you're bleedin'."

"Yes, Ma'am, I am."

"Is your horse hurt?"

"No," Clint aid, "he was smart enough to run off when I got shot. But we had to leave my saddle behind."

"You willin' to give up that gun on your hip if I help ya?" she asked.

Clint, who had been feeling pretty weak from the loss of blood for the past few miles, staggered a bit and said, "Yes, Ma'am . . ." At that point his legs gave out and he went down to one knee.

"Easy!" she said, rushing up to him. "All right, lemme help ya up."

She put her hand out and pulled him to his feet with surprising strength.

"You better lean on your horse," she said.

"Good idea."

"And let me have that gun."

He drew the gun and handed it to her, a movement which was alien to him. He rarely gave up his weapon, but there didn't seem to be any other way to get help.

"All right, then," she said, "let's get you in the house so I can see how bad that wound is."

Chapter Seventeen

She helped him into the house and to a chair at a wooden table. Eclipse stood patiently outside.

"Will I be able to water my horse?" he asked.

"You will," she said. "There's a well out back. But you'll have to wait until I patch you up." She went to her sink and pumped some water into a cup. "Here," she said, offering it to him.

"Thank you."

"Sit back. Let me get this shirt off."

The shirt, and the makeshift bandage, clung to the dried blood. As she tugged them free the wound began to seep again.

"In and out," she said, looking him over. "I'll have to clean both sides."

She got some more water, cleaned the wound, then made better bandages out of cloth and wrapped him up.

"There," she said. "If you don't move around a lot you may not bleed to death."

"I'm much obliged, Miss . . ."

"Just call me Delta," she said.

"That's a fine name," he said.

"It's what I go by."

"Well, thanks, Delta, but now I've got to see to my horse."

As he started to rise, she put a hand on his left shoulder and pushed him back down.

"You relax and drink some more water. I'll take your horse out back and water him, even rub him down. Then I'll come back and get you something to eat and some coffee."

"That sounds good."

"How long you been walkin'?" she asked.

"Just since this morning," he said.

"It'll be dark soon," she said. "I'll get your horse situated, then do the same for you."

"As long as we're not in the way," he said, looking around. "I don't want to put your husband or children out—"

"No husband, no kids," she said, "just me. And you will be puttin' me out, but it can't be helped. I couldn't just let ya bleed to death, and that's too fine a horse not to take care of."

"Thanks again," he said. "My name's Clint."

She put another cup of water in front of him and said, "Just sit still, Clint. I'll be back."

She went out the front, and he noticed she took her rifle and his gun with her.

***

Clint realized he had dozed off when Delta came back into the house.

"You wanna lay down or eat?" she asked him.

"Both," he said, "but I'd eat first."

"I got some dried meat and bread. I can make you a sandwich and some coffee."

"Sounds good," he said.

She put his gun down in the kitchen next to the sink, then leaned her rifle up against the nearby wall. She'd be able to grab either one if he tried something.

"That's some animal you got there," she said, while she cut two thick pieces of bread. "He just followed me around back. I didn't even have to coax him."

"He could probably smell the well," Clint said.

"Do I need to put a bridle on him and tie him off to keep him from wanderin'?"

"No," Clint said, "he'll be fine."

"That's what I thought you'd say."

She assembled the sandwich for him, brought it to the table with a cup of coffee. He started to wolf it down. She poured herself a cup of coffee, then sat across from him with her rifle.

"So who shot you?"

"A man I didn't expect it from," he said.

"A friend?"

"Not really, but we were traveling together."

"So he surprised ya?"

He nodded.

"In the morning, when I first woke up." He explained the situation to her.

"How's your arm now?" she asked.

He flexed it and said, "Working fine."

"The body's a funny thing," she said. "There's all kinda connections."

"I guess you're right." He finished the sandwich, washed it down with the coffee.

"Another one?" she asked.

"No, but I'll take more coffee."

She poured him another cup.

"Clint what?" she asked.

"Sorry?"

"You said your name's Clint," she said. "Clint what?"

"Adams," he said. "Clint Adams."

She stared at him, then stood up, got his gun from the kitchen counter, and handed it to him.

"You might as well have this back," she said. "I'm guessin' you coulda killed me out front any time you wanted to."

"Then I wouldn't 've had that sandwich," he told her, putting the gun in his holster. "I'm much obliged."

Chapter Eighteen

Clint started to slump down onto the table, so Delta got him to his feet and, with him leaning on her, walked him to her bed.

When he woke hours later, he stared at the ceiling, trying to remember where he was. He also looked around quickly for his gun, relaxed when he saw it hanging on the bedpost. Then he went back to trying to figure out where he was.

The woman who came through the door saved him the trouble. He recognized Delta, and it all came back to him—including the pain in his shoulder.

"How you feelin'?" she asked him.

"Weak," he said.

"That's because you need more food and water," she said. "Here." She handed him the cup of water she was holding, helped him raise his head to drink it. "I'm makin' supper. You'll feel better after a full meal."

"My horse . . ." he started.

"All taken care of," she said. "Brushed and fed."

"Thank you."

"You want me to bring a plate in here?"

"No, no, that'd be too much trouble," he said. "I'll come to the table. But I'll need to wash up."

"You can use the kitchen pump for that. I'll leave you a towel."

He drifted off to sleep again, but when she came in and woke him, he was ready to get to his feet. She helped him up, and he walked to the kitchen on his own, washed in the sink, then sat at the table. He had left his gun on the bedpost, which made him uncomfortable, but he felt that getting up to get it would make *her* uncomfortable. So he tried to put it out of his mind that his gun was not within reach. If someone broke in through the front door and killed him, he'd deserve it.

"This is a beef stew like you've never had before," she said, putting a steaming bowl in front of him.

"It smells great," he said.

She sat across from him and tucked into her own bowl. She had also put two large glasses of water on the table.

"Wow," he said, sitting back after his first bite.

"How is it?"

"Hot, spicy and delicious," he said.

"Oh, wait!" She got up and hurried back with a basket of biscuits. "I forgot these."

He grabbed a biscuit, broke it apart and used it to soak up some of the stew. The spiciness of it burned his mouth in the beginning, but he got used to it and started to eat avidly.

After he finished cleaning his bowl with another biscuit, she asked him if he wanted more.

"You bet!" he said, which seemed to please her. She got him another full bowl and then watched with great pleasure as he ate it.

"What about you?" he asked. "Or am I eating it all?"

"There's plenty," she said. "It's just been a long time since I watched a man eat at my table."

"How long have you lived out here alone?" he asked.

"Probably twenty years," she said.

"Where do you get your supplies?"

"There's a mercantile in a small town called Bottleneck, about five miles from here."

"Do they have a telegraph?" he asked.

"No," she said, "they ain't that big, yet. Why?"

"I just thought I might get some use out of it."

"Are you gonna look for the fella who shot you?"

"I am," he said. "I'm curious why he did it. Plus, I can't let the fact that he did do it go unpunished."

"Punished? You mean you're gonna kill 'im?"

"I think that's going to be up to him," Clint replied.

"Well," she said, "you ain't gonna be ready to travel for a while."

"I don't want to put you out anymore," he said. "I've already been a bother."

"Ain't no bother to have a man who eats like you in my house," she said, "or a horse that looks like that animal of yours out back."

He looked over at the wall, where she had hung her rifle up on a couple of hooks.

"How good are you with that rifle?"

"I'm good enough to keep people away from here," she assured him.

"You mean outlaws?"

"Outlaws, Injuns, the law," she said. "I don't care who they are as long as they stay away. You ain't gotta worry, I can keep ya safe while yer recoverin' here."

"I don't doubt it," he said. "Safe and well fed."

"Do you want some coffee?" she asked, grabbing his empty bowl.

"I would, very much," he said. "Thanks."

"You just sit there and relax," she said. "I noticed you lookin' over at yer gun hangin' on that bedpost. You want me to fetch it for ya?"

"No, that's all right. Like you said, I think I'm pretty safe here with you,"

Chapter Nineteen

Clint wanted to give Delta back her bed, but she insisted that he needed it more than she did. She had an old sofa she said she could bed down on. Reluctantly, he agreed.

He got a good night's sleep on her well-worn mattress and woke feeling stronger. She checked his wound in the morning, cleaned and bandaged it again, and then made breakfast.

She covered the table with eggs, bacon, potatoes, biscuits, butter, jam, and coffee.

"We can't eat like this every day," he said. "You're wasting your supplies on me."

"Gotta keep your strength up," she said. "Besides, I toldja I only gotta go about five miles to get more supplies."

He didn't know where she got her money and didn't feel he had the right to ask. But he could see she didn't farm, she didn't raise horses or cattle. He decided if she had to buy more supplies because he was there, he was going to offer her some money.

But he didn't plan to be there very long. He couldn't let C.W. Wellington get too much of a head start on him.

The man wouldn't be able to travel very fast with that wagon.

C.W.'s shooting him was a puzzlement. If the man wanted to kill him from the beginning, he could have done it when he put Clint in that coffin after drugging him. No, the decision to kill him must have come much later. Possibly just yesterday morning, on the spur of the moment.

Something happened to C.W. after the two of them got together. The only thing he could think of was the night Paul Sullivan came to his room, wanting to talk about Wellington. He had sent Sullivan down the hall to talk to C.W., who claimed the man never came. Now Clint was thinking that was a lie. The two men *had*, indeed, talked, and come to some sort of an agreement. Part of that agreement involved C.W. shooting Clint Adams.

Only he botched it. He was probably supposed to kill the Gunsmith, not just wound him. So now Clint was still alive and intended to find out what the grand plan was.

He stood up from the table and said, "I want to go out back and look at my horse."

"Of course," Delta said. "I ain't holdin' you prisoner."

First, he retrieved his gunbelt from her bedroom and strapped it on. Only then did he leave the house and walk around to the back, where Eclipse was standing. There was another horse back there, a buckboard, and a well.

Eclipse was standing easy. He turned his head and watched Clint approach. Delta had brushed his coat until he shone.

"Looking good, big fella," Clint said, walking around him. He examined all four of the Darley's legs, to make sure there were no injuries. "Seems like Delta's treated you about as well as she's been treating me."

He looked over at Delta's horse, who appeared to be a seven or eight-year-old mare. The buckboard had age on it but appeared solid enough to carry heavy loads.

Clint went to the well, got a bucket of water, then brought it back and allowed, first the mare to drink, and then Eclipse.

"Sorry," he told Eclipse, "but lady's first."

He took the bucket back to the well, then walked around to the front of the house. He stopped there to look off into the distance. The ground was flat and desolate enough for Delta to be able to see a long way. She must have seen him coming from a mile off.

He went back inside.

"How's he doin'?" she asked.

"He looks good," he said. "I watered them both."

"Daisy, too? Thanks. Are they gettin' along?"

"Eclipse seems to be ignoring her," Clint laughed. "That's pretty much how he treats everybody."

He sat down at the table. Walking behind the house and back had winded him.

"You need to take it easy," she told him. "How's the shoulder?"

"Stiff."

"And the arm?"

He flexed.

"It's working," he said. "I just hope it doesn't freeze up again at a time when I need it."

"I guess first chance you get you should see a doctor," she said. "Although I don't know what he'd do that I didn't do."

"Is there a doctor in . . . what did you say the town was . . . Bottleneck?"

"Yeah, that's it, and no, they don't have a doctor. People around tend to their own wounds."

"So that's how you knew what to do."

"Yes," she said, "you're not the first shootin' victim I've had to patch up."

"Yeah, you seemed very . . . confident."

"But like I said," she went on, "feel free to see a doctor first chance you get."

"I don't think I'll need to do that," he said. "I trust that you fixed me up."

"Good," she said, "then trust me when I say, you better get some more rest."

Chapter Twenty

Clint woke the next morning to the smell of bacon and coffee. He eased out of bed, took a few moments to try to loosen up. Mostly, he worked on his right arm, trying to make sure it had all its movement. It seemed to be working fine, so he stood up and walked into the other room.

"You're awake," she said. "Good. I don't have to wake you up to eat."

"The smells woke me," he said. "Did you sleep all right on the sofa?"

"I slept good," she assured him. "Have a seat and I'll get you some coffee."

He sat at the table and she set a cup in front of him.

"Thanks."

She went back to the stove, spoke to him from there. She was wearing a worn looking shirt and skirt, and some old boots.

"I thought I'd go to town today, get some supplies," she said.

"I'll go with you," he said.

"No." She turned and looked at him "You'll stay here. You shouldn't travel at all til you've rested longer and given your wound time to heal. I don't want you to undo everything I've done."

"Good point," he said, "but I'm going to give you some money."

"I ain't asked to be paid," she snapped.

"I know," he said. "I appreciate all your help, Delta, but if I'm going to be here any longer, I'd like to make a contribution. If it's all right with you."

"It's fine," she said, softening a bit. "I'll take it."

She brought a plate of bacon-and-eggs to the table, followed by a basket of biscuits.

"Why are biscuits always in a basket?" he asked, picking one up. "No matter where I eat."

"Because that's where they belong," she told him. "You eat while I hitch up the buckboard."

"Aren't you going to eat?"

"I did," she said, "while I was cookin'." She looked sheepish. "I couldn't wait."

"That's fine," Clint said.

"You go ahead now," she said. "I'll be right back."

She left to hitch her mare to the buckboard, and took her rifle with her.

He ate his breakfast, wondering how long he was going to have to be there. He'd been shot before, and each time the recovery took its own time—some short, some long. He wanted this one to be short. For that reason, he agreed to stay behind while Delta went to Bottleneck for supplies.

By the time she came back in, having hitched her horse to the buckboard and driven it around to the front, Clint had finished his breakfast.

"I shouldn't be long," she told him. "I suggest you just keep restin' yourself until I get back."

"Here." He held his hand out to her.

She walked over to him and took the money from his hand, then counted it.

"This is too much," she said.

"Get what you need, and a little more," he said. "Some oats for the horses would be good, too."

"All right," she said, putting the money in the pocket of her skirt, "I'll do that. I'll be back soon."

She went out the door and he watched from the window as she climbed aboard her buckboard, set her rifle down at her feet, and snapped the reins at Daisy, the mare. He continued to watch until she was out of sight.

After that he went back to the bedroom, reclined on the bed with no intention of actually falling asleep, and then drifted off.

Chapter Twenty-One

When Clint woke, Delta had not yet returned. He checked the time and saw she had left two hours earlier. Not enough time for him to worry about her. He probably shouldn't worry at all, because she seemed very capable of taking care of herself.

He went to the kitchen area and poured himself a cup of coffee. It was lukewarm, but he drank it. He put the cup down when he heard a horse outside—not a buckboard. He went to the front window and looked out. A man was approaching the house on horseback. He was alone, wearing buckskins with a feather in his hat.

"Delta, where the hell are ya?" he shouted. "You're usually out here by now, pointin' your rifle at me."

Clint went to the bedroom, picked up his gunbelt and strapped it on.

"Delta, gal!" the man shouted.

Clint opened the front door and stepped out. The man was still on horseback, holding a rifle in one hand. When he saw Clint, he brought the other hand around, so that he now had a two-handed grip.

"Take it easy," Clint said. "There's no call for gunplay."

"Where's Delta?"

"She went to Bottleneck for supplies," Clint said. "She's been gone two hours, so I expect she'll be back any minute. I'm assuming she's a friend of yours?"

"You her new man, or somethin'?" the man asked.

"No," Clint said. "I was wounded, and she helped me. That's all."

The man released his rifle with one hand.

"That sounds like her," he said. "She ain't the friendly type, but she *is* helpful."

"Am I going to get in trouble if I invite you in for a cup of coffee?"

"Not likely," the man said. "My name's Jake Lamb. Me and Delta been friends for years." Clint stared at him. "I'm a lot older than her. Met 'er when she was a little thing."

"You might as well come in, then," Clint said. "If you're lying, I assume she'll take care of you."

Lamb cackled and dismounted.

"Yep, she'd do that," he said, "if I was lyin'." He tied his horse off and followed Clint inside.

"The coffee needs to be heated," he said. "Take a few minutes."

"That's fine," Lamb said. "I'll jes' sit."

Clint lit the stove, then looked at Jake Lamb. Up close he could've been sixty or seventy, but he moved like a man much younger.

"What do you do, Mr. Lamb?"

"Ya'all jes' call me Jake, friend. I was a mountain man at one time, but these days I jes' hunt. Who're you?"

"My name's Clint Adams."

"Geez, I know who you are," Lamb said. "Who shot you?"

"It's a long story," Clint said. "It was somebody I thought was with me, turned out to be against me."

"So you gonna hunt 'im down?" Lamb asked.

"I am," Clint said, "as soon as I recover from this."

"Shoulder, huh?"

"Yep."

Clint poured two cups of coffee and took them to the table.

"There you go."

"Obliged," Lamb said.

As he sipped the hot coffee, they both heard the sound of a buckboard approaching.

"There she is," Lamb said. "I know the sound of that axle anywhere."

"Well, now I'll find out if I should've let you in or not," Clint said. "Maybe she'll get mad and shoot both of us."

"God, no," Lamb said. "I was hopin' to get some of her cookin'."

"Then maybe we should go out and help her unload," Clint said.

"You mean me," Lamb said, standing up. "You ain't liftin' nothin' with that shoulder."

They both went to the door and stepped out.

"Lamb, you old codger!" Delta shouted. "Help me unload this wagon."

"See?" Lamb said to Clint. "Friends."

He ran to the buckboard and began helping Delta unload her supplies and bring them into the house.

"You fellers introduce yourselves?" she asked.

"We did," Clint said.

"I'm Lamb," the older man said, "and he's the Gunsmith." He cackled. "You got yerself a fine new friend, Delta."

"You've got that wrong, Lamb," Clint said. "I'm the one with a fine new friend." He nodded to Delta.

"You got two new friends, Clint," Lamb said. "And you just call me Jake."

"All right, Jake."

It turned out Delta had a root cellar beneath the floor, and a lot of the supplies went there.

"Jake, if you're gonna stay for supper you might as well take the buckboard, my horse and your horse out back and see to them."

"Will do, Delta, girl, will do," Jake Lamb said, and went outside.

"He's an interesting character," Clint said.

"He's the closest thing I have to a father," Delta said. "How are you feelin'?"

"Stronger," he said.

"You'll need a few more days," she said, "then you can be on your way."

"If I can track down the man who shot me," he said, "I'll owe it all to you."

"Just don't get shot doin' it," she said.

"I'll sure try not to."

Chapter Twenty-Two

Delta prepared some chickens she had bought in Bottleneck and they all sat down to supper. While they ate, Clint told Jake about Caleb Wellington, the traveling undertaker, in case the man might have heard something about him.

"Why, ain't never heard of such a thing," he said, shaking his head. "A travelin' undertaker? Does he carry dead bodies in his wagon?"

"I suppose he would," Clint said. "I know he has coffins back there." He didn't tell them how he knew.

"Well, if that ain't the damndest thing I ever did hear," Jake said. "But even if I ain't heard a word about him, I don't guess he'd be too hard to find."

"Probably not," Clint said, "if he's still driving that wagon, pulled by Clydesdales."

"Now these Clyd—horses of his," Jake asked, "what're they like?"

Clint described the animals to him.

"Doesn't sound like they'd do me much good," the older man said.

"No," Clint said, "they're pretty much bred to pull a wagon."

"And leave a big trail to follow," Jake said. "You know, I could go with you and track 'em for you."

"Clint's not goin' anywhere for a while, yet," Delta said.

"I got it," Jake said, his fingers and face shiny with chicken grease. He put the meat down and licked his fingers clean. "Why don't I track 'em for ya while you're here, recoverin'? And by the time you're ready to go, I'll know where he is."

"That don't sound like a bad idea," Delta said.

"No, it doesn't," Clint said. "But I couldn't ask you to do that. Hell, we just met. Why would you do it?"

"'cause maybe I'm tired of huntin' animals?" Jake suggested. "And since you're a friend of Delta's, you're a friend of mine."

"He'll do it," Delta assured Clint. "He'll find him."

"Okay," Clint said, "that'll work."

"Just tell me where he was gonna go, what he was gonna do," Jake said.

"I know that information, but it may not be good anymore," Clint said. "I think something changed his mind."

"So tell me where to start," Jake said. "Where to pick up the trail."

"About half a day from here," Clint said, "to the west. You'll find the dead campfire, and the tracks made by the wagon and Clydesdales."

"Good," Jake said. "I'll head out tomorrow mornin'."

"You can bed down on the floor," Delta said. "I got the sofa, Clint's got the bed."

"No problem," Jake said, and picked up his chicken again.

***

Before turning in, Clint went around back to check on Eclipse. While he was there, he also looked at Daisy, Delta's mare, and Jake's pinto, who he called Dancer, "Because he's light on his feet."

"We're going to spend a few more days here getting some rest, big guy," Clint said to Eclipse. "And then we'll be on our way."

Eclipse looked at Clint and bobbed his big head up and down.

"He understands you," Jake said, from behind him.

"He does," Clint said. "We've been partners a long time."

"I've had Dancer for two years," Jake said. "But he's still kinda dumb."

"You refer to your horse as him," Clint said. "You're close to him."

"Only because we spend every day together," Jake said. "I've got nobody else to talk to, except when I come here to see Delta."

"She says you're the closest thing she's ever known to a father," Clint commented.

"And I kinda think of her as my daughter."

"How long have you known each other?"

"Forty years or so."

"And has she lived here all that time?"

"Yeah," Jake said. "Her parents died when she was young. Another family took her in but didn't treat her right. She left and found this house abandoned. She's been here ever since."

"How did you meet?"

"I used to squat here, sometimes," Jake said. "I came one day, and there she was. She said it was her house, now."

"And you let her have it?"

"She said it with a rifle," Jake added. "I was impressed. I told her she could have it, but I'd like to come by from time to time. That's been our relationship."

"Has she always been alone?"

"She's had a man here a few times," he said. "Always a different one."

"Where does she meet them?"

Jake shrugged.

"In town, or they come ridin' up. Sometimes she runs 'em off with her rifle, sometimes she don't. Like you."

"I'm lucky, then."

"Very," he said. "If you didn't already have a bullet in you, she woulda put one there."

Clint didn't bother pointing out that the bullet had gone right through.

"I'm going to turn in," Clint said. "Are you coming inside?"

"Naw," Jake said, "I figured I'd bed down out here with the horses. I can sleep on the back of the buckboard." He waved the blanket he was holding in one hand. "This is all I'll need." He had his rifle in his other hand. "And this."

"I'll see you in the morning, then," Clint said, "at breakfast."

"I'll get an early start on trackin' that travelin' undertaker of yours."

"I appreciate it."

"Hey," Jake said, "I'm obliged. It gives me somethin' different to do for a change."

Clint nodded, said good night, and went back inside the house.

Chapter Twenty-Three

The next morning Delta made then bacon-and-eggs, saying she wanted both of them fortified for what they had to do—Jake the tracking, and Clint the recovering.

Clint went out back to watch Jake saddle his horse and tell him as much as he could that might be helpful.

"If you happen to find him," he said, "don't go near him. He surprised the hell out of me when he shot me. I didn't think he had that in him."

"All right," Jake said. "I'll just find 'im, and then come back here and get you."

"That'll work."

They walked around to the front of the house, where Delta was waiting.

"Don't you get yourself shot, Jake Lamb," she called out to him.

"I'll do my best," Lamb said. "Come on, Dancer. We got some trackin' to do."

Clint stood next to Delta, and they watched Jake ride off until he was out of sight.

When they got back inside, Delta took out some money and held it out to Clint.

"I didn't use all of what you give me," she said.

"That's okay," he said. "Hang on to it til next time."

"I really don't need it," she said, putting the money down on the table.

"I don't see how you live, Delta," he said. "You don't farm, or raise livestock . . . what do you do to make a living?"

"Why do you need to know that?" she asked.

"Because I feel like I'm taking advantage of you," he explained. "A woman alone, struggling . . ."

"I may be alone, Clint," she said, "but I ain't strugglin'."

"I hope you're telling me the truth, and not just trying to make me feel better."

She studied him for a moment, then said, "Sit down."

He sat at the table. She sat across from him.

"I'll tell you how I pay for my supplies," she said, "but first you have to do somethin' for me."

"What's that?"

"You're right, I'm a woman alone," she said, "and I ain't had a poke in a long time."

"And by 'poke' you mean sex," he said, wanting to be sure.

"Yeah, sex." She colored slightly, stood up and turned her back. "Now I'm embarrassin' myself."

"Delta—"

She turned and faced him, a fierce look taking over her face.

"I've had a man from time to time, but I don't think none of them was decent," she said. "A real man. That's how you seem to me, Clint. Decent and real."

"Well," he said, "I'm flattered—"

"I know I ain't pretty," she said, "and I ain't young and fresh. Fact is, I could use a good bath. But I hate baths. And I'd only take one if somethin' special was gonna happen."

"Do you have a tub?" he asked.

She nodded.

"And buckets. I usually fill the bath from the well out back."

"Okay, then," he said, "why don't we start with that?"

"A bath?"

He nodded.

"And after that?"

He stood up and walked over to her. She was probably forty, but a hard life had etched lines into her face, making her look older. And she was right, she wasn't pretty, but neither was she unpleasant to look at.

"And I'll wash your back," he said, "among other things . . ."

Chapter Twenty-Four

The bathtub was behind the house, against the wall. Clint had noticed it earlier but had not really thought about it. He started to lift it to take it inside, but his shoulder wouldn't let him.

"Lemme do it," Delta said.

He watched as she dragged the tub inside. Then, instead of filling it from the well, she got the water from the pump in the sink. After she filled it, she boiled some water on the stove and dumped that in. The whole time Clint sat and watched her move around. He found himself wondering what she was going to look like with her clothes off.

"There," she said. "It's all set."

"Good," he said. "Get in."

"We're gonna need soap, and a towel," she said, rushing around the room.

"Delta, are you nervous?"

She stopped in her tracks and looked at him.

"Yeah, I'm nervous."

"Well, don't be," Clint said. "Right now you're just going to take a bath. You don't have to do anything else after that."

"I want to," she said. "I want to do . . . a lot."

"Then maybe I should get in the tub with you," he offered.

"Oh, no," she said. "You're gonna keep that bandage dry. I'm getting into the tub alone."

"All right, then," he said. "Do it before the water cools off."

"Right."

She hesitated, then stepped to the tub, turned her back to Clint and dropped her dress. She was naked underneath. Her butt had more curve to it than he had suspected. Her skin was pale where the sun never got to it, and almost brown where the sun baked her face and arms. He watched her long legs as she stepped into the tub and settled into the water.

"All right," Clint said, "time for the soap."

He stood, picked up the soap and a cloth and went to the tub. She sat in an almost hunched position, arms folded across her chest, as he crouched down next to her.

"Come on, Delta," he said, "this was what you wanted. Just relax your shoulders."

She did, with some effort, and then she lowered her hands. Her breasts were small, the nipples aroused by the water. He reached in and started to soap her back, using his hands rather than a cloth.

Delta closed her eyes as he washed her back, her shoulders, even ran his hand down to the top of the clef between her butt cheeks.

"That's good," he said, "now you're relaxing."

"Really?" she asked. "I feel like I'm gettin' . . . excited."

"Then . . . you want me to do your front?"

She leaned back in the tub and said, "Please."

He started to soap up the cloth and she said, "You don't need the cloth."

He began to soap her throat, and shoulders, and then her breasts. They felt surprisingly firm beneath his palms, and her nipples felt as if they were going to scrape his skin.

Delta moaned as he continued to rub the soap and his hands over her chest.

"It's been a long time since a man touched me like this," she said.

"Really?" he asked, moving his hand further down until it was between her legs. He moved his fingers through her thick, wet bush until he found her heat, which was hotter than the water.

"Omigod," she gasped, as he slipped one finger, and then two, inside of her.

He used the two fingers, as well as his thumb, to push her over the edge. As waves of pleasure overtook her, she lost control of her legs, which thrashed around in the tub, spilling much of the water onto the floor. As she let her head drop back, her body finally relaxed. He used the rest of the water to wash her long legs before he started to lift her out of the tub. His intention was to carry her into the bedroom, but it was as if she suddenly came awake at that point.

"No!" she snapped. "You'll hurt your shoulder. I'll walk."

He helped her from the tub, and her legs almost buckled beneath her.

"Give me a few seconds," she said, leaning on his uninjured side. "I told you it's been a while, and my legs are still trembling."

"That's all right," Clint said. "We've got plenty of time."

"I'm ready," she said, and they walked to the bedroom together. Once they got there, Clint used the towel to dry her off before she got into bed. Then she watched as he undressed so he could join her.

"Oh Lord," she said, as his hard dick came into view.

She reached out to take him in one hand and stroke him. But then she tightened her grip and pulled on him so he'd join her in bed.

Chapter Twenty-Five

In bed, Delta came alive.

There was no blushing, no shyness, no hunched shoulders. She pushed Clint down on his back, then knelt alongside him and explored his body with her hands and mouth.

"It's been a long time," she told him, "so I'm, gonna go slow."

"Go as slow as you want," he said.

And she did. When she reached his hard penis, she spent a lot of time there, rubbing it over her face, stroking it, licking it up and down, until she finally opened her mouth and took it in. She sucked it slowly, working it in and out of her mouth, moaning as she did so. There was nothing whorish in what she was doing, as some might have thought. No, this was a woman who had sex infrequently, and when she did, wanted to experience it fully. And enjoy it.

He didn't know how much longer he'd be with her, or how many more times they'd do this. So he decided to just let her go.

He closed his eyes and enjoyed the sensations of her hands and mouth on him. For a woman who hadn't had sex in a long time, she seemed very confident in what she was doing.

But as much as he wanted to let her have her way, he thought he wasn't going to be able to hold back much longer, so he reached down for her.

"Jesus," he said, "come on up here before it's too late."

She obliged, climbing up on him, then settling down and taking his long cock inside of her.

"Oh God, yes," she said, moving her hips in a circular motion as her heat closed around him. "Oh, Jesus."

He moved his hips with her, fascinated by the rapturous expression on her face. He had been with many women who enjoyed their time with him, but never quite like this . . .

***

Jake Lamb found the campsite Clint had described to him. He dismounted and studied the tracks left by the wagon and the Clydesdales. They were impressive and would not be difficult to follow.

He mounted Dancer and started following the trail. He was able to see how much Delta liked Clint Adams, so he was doing this mostly for her, rather than for him. Although it sure wouldn't hurt to have a man like the Gunsmith indebted to him.

***

Delta slept with her head on Clint's left shoulder. Although his right one was still sore, his arm was free, in case he needed to go for his gun. Although out in the middle of nowhere it didn't seem likely anyone would be able to sneak up on them.

She stirred, then removed her head from his shoulder.

"Am I hurtin' you?" she asked.

"Not at all," he said. "I'm very comfortable."

"How could you be comfortable with somebody lyin' on ya?" she asked, laughing. "Are you hungry?"

"Somehow," he said, "I've managed to build up an appetite."

"So have I," she said, sliding off the bed. She walked naked across the room, and he watched her with pleasure. Now that the shyness between them was gone, she was a self-assured, mature woman. She opened a dresser drawer, took out a robe and put it on.

"How about some eggs?" she asked.

"Sounds perfect."

"You relax," she said. "I'll come and get you when it's ready."

"What about moving the tub—"

"I can handle that," she said. "Don't worry."

She left the room and soon he heard her bustling around the kitchen.

***

When he got dressed and came out of the bedroom, she had food on the table. It was more than eggs, and enough to feed an army.

"Jesus," he said.

"You need to keep your strength up."

"I know," he said, "especially after what we just did."

They sat down across from each other and both began to eat voraciously.

"I have to thank you," she said.

"For what?"

"For not turning around and runnin' away when I mentioned sex."

"Why would I run?"

"Most men would've."

"I didn't find it off-putting, Delta," he said. "I enjoyed it."

"So did I," she said. "Can we do it again?"

"I think so," he said, "but let's finish eating first, all right?"

***

Three days later, Clint and Delta got out of bed, had breakfast, and then she walked him outside and watched him saddle Eclipse.

"Are you sure you feel up to ridin'?" she asked.

"It's time, Delta."

"I thought you'd want to wait for Lamb to come back with some information," she said.

"That would've been nice," Clint said, "but I'll probably run into him, out there."

"So where are you gonna start?" she asked, as they walked Eclipse around to the front. "Are you gonna track him from your last campsite?"

"No," Clint said, "we were going to Cody when C.W. shot me. I think I'll head in that direction."

"You think he'd still go there?"

"I don't know," Clint said. "I never thought he'd shoot me, so I can't predict his movements with any confidence."

She gave him a hug and he mounted up.

"Is there any chance you'd come back here when it's all over?" she asked.

"I don't think so, Delta," Clint said.

"I understand," she said.

111

"I owe you my life," he said. "Thank you."

"Just . . . don't get shot again," she told him.

"I'll do my best."

He rode away, and she stayed out in front of the house until he was out of sight.

Chapter Twenty-Six

Clint rode into Cody two days later, having not pushed himself or Eclipse. It was unlikely he'd find Caleb Wellington there, so why rush? All he wanted to find out was if C.W. ever *was* there, and if anyone knew where he might have been going next.

Since C.W. was so noticeable with his wagon and Clydesdales, Clint decided to go straight to the sheriff's office and see what he could learn. As it turned out, Cody had a town marshal. He stopped in front of the office and dismounted.

As he entered, three men turned and looked at him. They were all wearing badges, but the older man in the center—who looked to be in his fifties—was wearing the marshal's badge. The other two were deputies.

"Sorry," Clint said, "am I intruding?"

"Hell, no," the marshal said. "I'm just tellin' my deputies to get the hell out of my office and go do their jobs." He looked at the two younger men. "Go!"

"Yessir," they said, and left.

"I'm Marshal John Butler," the man said. "What can I do for you?"

"Marshal," Clint said, "my name's Clint Adams."

"The Gunsmith?"

"That's right," Clint said, "and I'm not here looking for trouble."

"Well, Mr. Adams," Butler said, "it seems to be you're the kind of fella who pretty much has trouble find him."

"You've got that right."

"Have a seat and tell me what brings you to Cody," Butler invited.

They both sat, Butler behind an unimpressive desk. It was nice to see a man who didn't worry about the size of his desk.

"I'm looking for a man named Caleb Wellington."

"Wellington?" Butler frowned.

"You'd remember him," Clint said. "He fancies himself a traveling undertaker."

Butler snapped his fingers and pointed.

"Big wagon, ugly horses?" he asked.

"That's him."

"Yeah, yeah," Butler said, "he was here."

"He was? How along ago?"

"A week, maybe ten days."

It was probably more like ten days since Clint had been with Delta for about five.

"You said he was here," Clint said. "That means he's not now."

"No," Butler said, "he left town, was only here a couple of days, I think."

"Did he do any business while he was here?" Clint asked.

"You mean did he bury anybody?" Butler asked. "No, we have a town undertaker for that."

"So what did he do?" Clint asked.

"Beats me," the lawman said. "I really didn't pay that much attention to him. I mean, what with the bank robbery, and all."

"Bank robbery?"

"Yeah," Butler said. "The Wyoming National was hit around that time."

"At the same time he was in town?"

"Yeah," Butler said. "Three men held it up."

"Did they shoot anybody?"

"No, they managed it without firing a shot."

"And was anybody able to identify them?" Clint asked.

"No, they had their faces covered," Butler said. "I got a posse together real quick and we chased 'em. Caught 'em, too."

"You caught the bank robbers?"

"Well," Butler said, "we caught up to three men, but they didn't have any money on them, so we hadda let 'em go. Too bad, too, because I just heard that it happened again."

"Where?"

"In a town not far from here."

"And when was this?"

"A couple of days ago," Butler said. "It's odd, we went a long time without any crimes in this area, and now we've had two bank robberies, and a murder."

"A murder? Who was murdered?"

"An old timer who rode in here about five days ago," Butler said.

"Who was he?"

"We didn't get a name," Butler said, "but he was dressed like a mountain man, in buckskins."

"Marshal," Clint said, "can we go over all of this again, very slowly?"

Chapter Twenty-Seven

Clint looked sadly upon the prone body of Jake Lamb, in the undertaker's office. He was wrapped in a blanket and had to be unwrapped for Clint to view him.

"He was killed days ago?" Clint asked. "Why hasn't he been buried?"

"Uh, there was no one to pay for the service, sir," the undertaker said.

"Well, you get his body in a box and plant him, and I'll pay for it," Clint said.

"Yessir."

Clint left the undertaker's, found the marshal waiting out front.

"Is that your friend?" the man asked.

"That's him," Clint said. "Who killed him?"

"We don't know," Marshal Butler said. "He was found out by the livery. Somebody cut his throat."

"And was that traveling undertaker in town when it happened?"

"I think so."

"And had the bank been robbed?"

Butler scratched the stubble on his jaw.

"I'm gettin' pretty confused about the order of things, to tell the truth," he admitted. "Two bank robberies and a murder, I didn't really keep track of that undertaker's wagon."

"Where was the second bank robbery?"

"About ten miles from here, a town called Millard."

"Same thing? Three men?"

"Yep. The sheriff there got a posse together, but couldn't catch up to them."

"And was the traveling undertaker there, too?"

"That I don't know," Butler said. "Why, what're you thinkin'?"

"I'm thinking that big wagon would be a perfect hiding place for the stolen money, or even the bank robbers, themselves."

"I reckon you could be right."

"I'm going to be here overnight," Clint said. "Is there a telegraph in Millard?"

"No."

"Can you send someone to find out if the wagon was there when the bank was robbed."

"Sure can," Butler said. "Like I said, it's only about ten miles away."

"Great," Clint said. "I appreciate it. I've got to go back inside and pay for my friend's burial, but then I'll find a hotel."

"Check out the Cody House," Butler said. "Best place in town."

"Thanks."

Butler headed off and Clint went back inside.

***

Clint got himself a room at the Cody House, dropped his saddlebags and rifle onto the table and sat on the bed. He felt terrible. Lamb had been in Cody because of him, because he tracked the wagon there, so it was his fault the man was dead. He didn't know how he was going to tell Delta. But before he could do that, he'd have to catch up with Caleb Wellington and find out who he was working with, and who killed Lamb.

He could only come up with one name, and that was Sullivan. He couldn't think of anyone else C.W. had spoken to. Could it be possible that a sheriff and an undertaker were robbing banks? And they had drafted C.W. into service because of his wagon?

It seemed to Clint he was going to have to go back to Venture, not so much to find C.W., but to find out if the little Brit had conspired with the Sullivans. The only problem was, he wouldn't be able to just ride back in. He was going to have to get there without being seen, find out if C.W.'s wagon was there, and maybe get a look inside. Also check out the Sullivan brothers. It would be a pretty clever plan for them to be robbing banks in the area, and then just return to their town to do their jobs.

He'd lost track of how long he'd been sitting there. Even though he was heartsick over the death of Jake Lamb, Clint found that he was hungry. He decided to go down to the Cody House dining room and get something to eat.

***

He ordered a steak supper and took his time eating it. There was no rush. He just needed the answer to that one question from the sheriff, and then he could turn in with intentions of riding out early the next morning.

He was having a slice of pie for desert when the sheriff walked in and approached his table.

"Mind if I join you?"

Why did lawmen always ask that, when they were going to sit no matter what?

"Have a seat," Clint said. "Coffee?"

"Sure."

Clint poured him a cup from his pot.

"Well," Butler said. "I got the answer to your question."

"Already?"

"The kid I sent over to Millard rode like hell and came back with some information."

"Which is?"

"That traveling undertaker was there when the bank was robbed."

"I figured."

"What do you plan to do now?"

"I've got an idea of where these bank robbers are based," Clint said. "I'm going to head there and see what I can find out."

"I'd go with you, but I'd be out of my jurisdiction, there. You'll have to depend on the local law."

Clint didn't bother pointing out that depending on the local law might be a problem.

"Thanks for your help, Marshal."

"Thanks for the coffee."

The marshal left and Clint returned to his room.

***

In the morning, when he collected his horse from the livery, he came out and found the marshal waiting for him.

"I thought you'd want your friend's belongings," he said, handing Clint some things that belonged to Jake

Lamb. There wasn't much, but he stuffed them into his saddlebags so he could give them to Delta, at some point.

"Appreciate it, Marshal."

"And I'll see that the burial gets done, just like you paid for it."

"Again," Clint said, "thanks."

"We got a telegraph here in Cody," the man told Clint. "Let me know what happens. We'd like to get some of that bank money back."

"I'll do the best I can," Clint said. He mounted up and rode out.

Chapter Twenty-Eight

The ride to Venture took a day. Again, he didn't push. It seemed as if the bank robbers were having a lot of luck, so they wouldn't be looking for any trouble, and certainly wouldn't be going anywhere. He wanted them to be nice and relaxed and overconfident when he got there. Unless, of course, they were out robbing another bank. Then he'd have to wait for them to return.

He camped the first night when he probably could've snuck in but decided to take the next day to surveille the small town. Certainly, if C.W.'s wagon was there it would stick out, unless they were hiding it.

He made a cold camp meal out of water and beef jerky, then took to his bedroll for a night's sleep. It was fitful, but he knew he could rely on Eclipse to warn him if anyone was approaching.

He woke in the morning with his shoulder stiff. He decided to make coffee, since a fire glow wouldn't be seen in the daylight, but he was careful to keep it from billowing too much smoke. Winter was in the offing, and the coffee warmed his insides. He also took some time to stretch his injured shoulder, trying to work out the stiffness, and keep his right arm mobile.

There was plenty of high ground around the town of Venture, so he was pretty much able to circle the town and get a good look at it. He saw the sheriff coming and going to his office, and one time actually stopping at his brother's undertaker's office. Another time he saw the undertaker, Paul Sullivan, go to the saloon. With the use of a spy glass, he was able to recognize the man as the one who had come to his room.

But he didn't see anything that might indicate Caleb Wellington was there. For that he was going to have to take a closer look. C.W.'s wagon and team might have been hidden inside the livery stable.

Clint decided to leave Eclipse on his own, knowing he wouldn't go anywhere, and slip into town, behind the livery to get a look. It would have been easier to do it in the dark, but then the livery might have been locked.

There wasn't much happening on the streets of the small town. He just waited until he knew where both Sullivan's were—the sheriff in his office, the undertaker in the saloon—before making his way down to the livery.

When he reached the stable, he flattened his back against the wall and waited a few moments to see if anyone raised an alarm. There was a corral, but no horses for him to worry about spooking. There were no wagon or Clydesdale tracks in the dirt, but the wagon would've had to be driven into the livery from the front. He didn't want to risk going to the front, so he simply went to the small back door and checked to see if it was unlocked. It was. He opened it slowly, just in case there was somebody inside. When he had it open just wide enough for his head, he took a look. There was nobody around, but C.W.'s wagon was right in the center, and the Clydesdales were each in a stall.

He opened the door wider and slipped inside.

There were several other horses in stalls as well as the Clydesdales. But they were all standing calmly, ignoring him. He went to the wagon, tried the doors in the back and found them unlocked. He opened them and climbed in. There was still a coffin right in the center, probably the one he had been in when C.W. drugged him. He gripped the lid tightly, then lifted it slowly. With great satisfaction, he saw money bags from not only two banks, but three. He opened the lid of the coffin all the way so he could use both hands to look inside the bags. They were still stuffed with stacks of bills. One bag, from a bank in a town he'd never heard of, was filled with loose bills that had been tossed in, probably in a hurry.

He was about to close the lid of the coffin when an idea occurred to him. All he needed was enough time to get it done.

***

Clint made his way up the slope to where he had left Eclipse. He mounted up and rode back to where he had camped the night before. The embers of his fire were still hot, and he had left the coffee pot there. He poured himself a cup and hunkered down to do some thinking.

He had a new plan, but it meant riding back into town, right down the main street. No sneaking and no hiding. He was pretty sure that the Sullivan brothers would go along with his request and turn Caleb Wellington over to him. They could keep the man's wagon and team, and still run their bank robbery ring out of it. They didn't need C.W. to make it all work.

He wondered what C.W. had told them about shooting him. Had that been a plan they'd all hatched? Or had C.W. decided to do it all on his own. It seemed to Clint that the little Brit had acted on the spur of the moment. Thank God he hadn't taken the time to calmly aim. If the Sullivans weren't part of the shooting, maybe they wouldn't be happy about it. After all, shooting Clint and not killing him had managed to bring him right back here. And *that* certainly would not have been a part of the Sullivan's plan.

Chapter Twenty-Nine

Clint broke camp, doused the fire, spread the embers and packed his coffee pot. It was time to go. He wondered what the Sullivan's first reaction would be seeing him ride in, and how they'd play it? He had the feeling they wouldn't just start shooting, but he was ready if they did. He really didn't want to kill them until he knew where Caleb Wellington was.

He mounted up and headed down to town . . .

***

Paul Sullivan had just stepped out of the saloon and crossed the street when he saw a man riding in. He ducked into his brother's office.

"What is it?" Sheriff Sullivan asked. "You look like you've seen a ghost."

"Adams."

"What about 'im?"

"He's ridin' in."

"Are you sure?"

"I just saw 'im."

The lawman went to the window and looked out.

"Yeah, that's him, all right."

"What do we do?"

"What do you wanna do?"

"I wanna not get killed, Tom."

Tom Sullivan looked at his brother.

"Why would you get killed, Paul?" he asked. "Did you do anythin' to him?"

"No . . ."

"Did I do anythin' to him?"

"No . . ."

"Then stop worryin'."

"But what's he want? Why's he back here?"

"I'm gonna go out and ask 'im," Sheriff Sullivan said. "If you want, just wait here."

"Yeah," Paul Sullivan said, "that's what I'm gonna do."

Sheriff Tom Sullivan shook his head at his older brother, opened the office door and stepped out.

***

Clint had passed the sheriff's office, and had seen Paul Sullivan duck in there as he rode in. When the door opened, he was aware and looked back. The sheriff stepped out and actually waved to him.

He turned Eclipse and rode back to the man.

"Howdy, Adams," Sheriff Sullivan said. "Never expected to see you back here in our little one-horse town."

"Well, I never expected to come back here," Clint said. "But I'm looking for somebody."

"Who would that be?"

"Caleb Wellington."

"Who?"

"The fella I was here with last time," Clint said. "The traveling undertaker."

"And what would he be doin' back here?" Sullivan asked. "We told him we had an undertaker."

"That's true, you did," Clint said, "but I have a feeling you told him a whole lot more than that."

Sullivan frowned.

"I don't get your meanin'."

"I think you do, Sheriff," Clint said. "I think your brother, the undertaker, had a conversation with the little guy. I mean, he came to see me, but then he went down the hall to see C.W. and I think something got cooked up between them."

"Between your undertaker and mine?" the sheriff asked, laughing. "I don't think so."

"Is your brother around?" Clint asked. "I'd like to talk to him."

"Why don't you wait in the saloon across the street," the sheriff suggested, "and I'll find 'im and bring him to you there."

"Fine," Clint said, "I'll do that."

"It shouldn't take long," the lawman said.

He turned and went back into his office, while Clint rode Eclipse across to the saloon.

Chapter Thirty

Sheriff Sullivan went back into his office, immediately looked out the window.

"What'd he want? What'd he say?" Paul Sullivan demanded.

"He wants you."

"What?"

"Relax," the sheriff said. "He just wants to talk to you."

"So what'd you tell him.?"

"To go to the saloon and have a drink, and I'd bring you over."

"What? What am I supposed to say to him?"

"Just listen to his questions, and then lie," Sheriff Sullivan told his brother. "You know how to lie, don't ya?"

"Hell," Paul Sullivan said, "I taught you, didn't I?"

"Then just do what you're good at, Paul," the sheriff said. "Come on."

They both left the office and walked across the street to the saloon.

***

When the Sullivan brothers came walking into the saloon, Clint was at the bar working on a beer. There were three other men in the place, and the bartender. Clint had no idea how many of them he might have to go against.

"Mr. Adams," the sheriff said, "my brother, Paul."

"I know your brother," Clint said. "He came to my room and introduced himself."

"Ah, that's right, you said that. Paul?"

"Mr. Adams," Paul Sullivan said, "what can I do for you?"

"Well, first you and your brother can have a beer with me," Clint invited.

"I don't know about my brother," the sheriff said, "but I accept."

"Sure," the undertaker said, "why not?"

"Bartender," Clint said, "three beers, please."

"Comin' up, sir."

The barman set the three mugs on the bar, and then stepped back. That suited Clint. It meant the man wasn't within easy reach of a shotgun beneath the bar.

Clint and the Sullivans lifted their mugs and had a drink.

"Now maybe you can tell us what brings you back here, Mr. Adams," the lawman said.

"I'm looking for the traveling undertaker."

"I thought you were traveling together the last time you were here," Sheriff Sullivan said.

"We were," Clint said. "But that changed."

"When did that happen?" the lawman asked.

"When he shot me."

"What?" That seemed to amuse the sheriff.

"Why would he do that?" Paul Sullivan asked.

"Maybe," his brother said, "he was tryin' to drum up some business for himself."

"Well," Clint said, "he didn't do a very good job of it, did he? So now I'm lookin for him."

"To kill 'im?" the sheriff asked.

"To talk to him," Clint said.

"About what?" the sheriff asked.

"About who put him up to shooting me."

"You don't think he did it on his own?" the lawman asked.

"That's what I'm going to ask him," Clint said.

"And then you'll kill 'im."

"You're the law, Sheriff," Clint said. "I wouldn't tell you if that was what I was planning to do, would I?"

"I guess not."

"So whataya need me for?" Paul Sullivan asked.

"You spoke with him after you left my room."

"Did I?"

"You tell me," Clint said.

This would be interesting, because the undertaker didn't know what C.W. had told Clint. The Brit undertaker said they didn't talk. Whatever Sullivan told him, one of them would probably be lying.

"I did go down the hall to talk to him," Paul Sullivan said, "but when I knocked on the door there was no answer. I assumed he wasn't inside and left."

Okay, so now both men claimed they hadn't talked. Clint's logic that one of them was lying went out the window, because they could've both been lying, or both been telling the truth.

"Why?" Paul asked. "Did he say we did talk?"

"We didn't discuss it," Clint lied.

"What makes you think he'd come back here, anyway?" Sheriff Sullivan asked. "If he shot you, and knows he didn't kill you, he'd be on the run. Wouldn't he be far away from here?"

"He might," Clint said. "But since this was the last town I saw him in, I just thought I'd start here."

"Well," the sheriff said, "he ain't here. Now what?"

"There are still tracks outside from his wagon and horses," Clint said.

"Are there?" Sheriff Sullivan asked. "We don't get much traffic here. That could be from the time you were both here."

"I think it rained at least once since then," Clint said. "If you don't mind, Sheriff," Clint went on, "I'll just have a look around town, after I get myself a hotel room."

Sheriff Sullivan didn't flinch when he said, "Be my guest."

***

After Clint Adams left the saloon to get himself a hotel room Paul Sullivan said, "Are you crazy, tellin' him to go ahead and look around town?"

"He's goin' to the hotel first," the sheriff said. "You get your ass over to the livery and move that wagon and team."

"By myself?"

"No," the sheriff said, "get help, damn it. But leave Cleon in the livery to take care of Adams' horse."

"Ah, shit," Paul said, literally running from the saloon.

***

Clint had purposely told the Sullivan brothers that he was going to the hotel first. That would give them time to run and move C.W.'s wagon, and maybe even tell C.W.

that Clint was in town. He was holding back on suggesting they look in the wagon for their money.

That was his ace in the hole.

Chapter Thirty-One

Clint checked into the hotel and took the time to bring his saddlebags and rifle to his room. He also took his time coming back down and walking over to the livery. When he reached it, the front doors were wide open. He could see that the heavy tracks of the wagon had been brushed away in haste.

The hostler met him at the doors, which was a dead giveaway that he knew Clint was coming.

"Fine lookin' animal," the man said.

"Got room for him?" Clint asked.

"Plenty." The man took Eclipse's reins from Clint. "Stayin' long?"

"A day or two," Clint said, "no longer."

"I'll take good care of 'im," the man promised.

"What's your name?" Clint asked.

"Cleon."

"Much obliged, Cleon."

Clint turned and left the livery. The wagon tracks had been brushed away all the way to the street, but he was able to pick them up further on. They had apparently taken the wagon and the Clydesdales out of town. He decided not to follow the tracks. He could do that later, if he hadn't found C.W. by then.

He headed back toward the hotel but detoured to enter the saloon once again. Neither of the Sullivans were there. The three men inside watched him approach the bar.

"Back so soon?" the bartender asked.

"Long walk to the livery," Clint commented. "I need another beer."

"Comin' up."

The barman set a frothy beer down.

"Thanks," Clint said, picking it up. "Quiet town."

"We got us a good sheriff," the bartender said. "Keeps the peace."

"Good to know." Clint looked around the saloon. The three men, each seated at their own table, turned their eyes away.

"A town this big usually has more action," Clint commented."

"Whataya lookin' for?"

"Poker? Girls?"

The bartender shook his head.

"Nothin' like that. Sorry. That's why we don't get many visitors. It may look big, but there's nothin' much goin' on in this town."

"Might as well drink my beer and go to my room," Clint said. "I've got a good book to read."

But he nursed the beer. There was no hurry. He wanted the Sullivans to get nervous.

***

Paul Sullivan ran into his brother's office.

"You get it moved?" the sheriff asked.

"Yeah," Paul said, "the wagon and the horses."

"Where'd you put them?"

"The old Dillon place, outside of town."

"Brush the tracks away?"

Paul hesitated.

"Paul?"

"I did," the undertaker said.

"All the way?"

"Well, no . . . just in town."

"Stupid!"

"You think he's gonna go lookin' outta town?" Paul asked.

"He's the goddamned Gunsmith," the sheriff said. "He didn't live this long with that reputation by doin' things halfway."

"Why don't we just give him that little undertaker?" Paul suggested.

"We might," Sheriff Tom Sullivan said. "Let's just save that."

"So whatta we do in the meantime?"

"We lay low, and see what Adams does," the sheriff said. "Unless you want to go up against the Gunsmith?"

"Hell, I ain't never wanted to do that," Paul said. "You made me go to his room that time."

"Before we got that little traveling undertaker on our side," the sheriff pointed out. "Look, you can see the saloon and the hotel from your place. Go on over there and see if you spot where the Gunsmith is going."

"That's fine with me," Paul said. "I'd just as soon be in my place. At least I got a gun there."

"You can't carry a gun, Paul," the sheriff said. "That don't look right for an undertaker."

"You let me carry a gun when we pull jobs," Paul pointed out.

"That's because bank robbers need guns," Tom Sullivan said, "and undertakers don't. Now git."

"When did you become the boss, little brother?" Paul demanded.

"The first time I put on this badge," the sheriff said, "remember?"

"Yeah, yeah," Paul said, "I remember."

He turned and walked out of the office, leaving Sheriff Tom Sullivan to his own thoughts on how to handle the situation.

Chapter Thirty-Two

Clint actually found himself able to slip back into *Gulliver's Travels* for a while. Hell, there was nothing else to do, and he was waiting for darkness to fall so he could sneak around again. Of course, if one of the Sullivans got nervous enough to talk to him, that would help.

He didn't think the sheriff was particularly the nervous type. He seemed to be the youngest brother, but it was Paul, the undertaker, who appeared the most skittish. Clint knew the undertaker's office was right across the street, and even thought he'd been able to see the man peeking out his window as he walked from the saloon to the hotel.

The only other people he had interacted with in town were the bartender, the hotel clerk, and the hostler. The clerk was the most nervous of those. The bartender and hostler seemed calm enough. Apparently, they both felt confident that their sheriff could handle things.

Clint sat on the bed with the book in his hands, his gun close by, and the back of a wooden chair shoved underneath the doorknob.

He felt in control.

***

Paul Sullivan was sitting in the window of his office with his gun in his lap. He had never fired it in his life. He left that—when it was necessary—to his brother. Having Clint Adams in town was unnerving. If he'd had any confidence in his ability with a rifle, he might have just picked the man off from there when he came out of his hotel.

When Adams had been in his hotel for a while, he decided to go back to the sheriff's office. He took the gun with him, but stuck it in his belt behind his back, so his brother wouldn't see.

***

Sheriff Tom Sullivan wasn't happy when the door of his office opened and his brother came in, again.

"What now, Paul?"

"I just wanted to let you know he's in the hotel and has been for a while."

"Good," the lawman said. "He can stay there, and you can stay in your office."

"What are you gonna do?"

"I'm thinkin' about movin' that wagon," Tom said. "I don't like where you put it."

"Ya want me to help ya?"

"No," the sheriff said, "I'll take Cleon. You just stay put."

"Yeah, okay."

When Paul turned, he was sure his jacket covered the gun, but his brother said "And don't come outside with that gun on you again! You'll get yourself killed."

Paul left in a hurry.

***

Clint didn't complain when he got a room with a window that overlooked the street. He was able to see Paul Sullivan leave his office, rush to the sheriff's office, and then rush back. The man was very nervous, that was obvious.

The sheriff seemed satisfied to remain in his office. So the only question remaining was, where the hell was Caleb Wellington?

Chapter Thirty-Three

Clint closed his book when it got dark outside. He turned up his lamp so that anybody watching his window would think he was still there. He went to the door, removed the chair from the doorknob, and stepped into the hall. Luckily, the hotel had a back stairway to a rear door, so he didn't have to go past the desk clerk to leave.

Once he was outside, behind the hotel, he saw that he could pretty much move along the entire street from there. He knew that the wagon and team had been moved from the livery and taken out of town. Since no one had been nervous enough to talk to him, he decided to follow the tracks and see if C.W. was also in the same place.

The moon was high, which gave Clint plenty of light to see the heavy wagon tracks. He followed them out of town, but after only a few hundred yards, he heard something and stopped. It was that noisy axle of C.W.'s big wagon. Apparently, it was being moved again. He continued on toward the sound, moving very carefully.

When he reached an old house, he saw Sheriff Sullivan and the hostler, Cleon, working together to move the wagon and team, which they had hitched up. Apparently, the sheriff didn't like where his brother had left it. The wagon was noisy enough that he was able to follow them with no trouble, hoping they would lead him to C.W.

They seemed to be going a pretty long way, but he could see lights from town and knew they were walking parallel to it. Wherever they were taking the wagon, they would still be able to walk back to town.

Finally, they came to what looked like an old barn and walked the team and wagon inside. Apparently, the front doors were not as old as the rest of the structure, and they closed and locked them.

"That should do it," he heard the sheriff say.

"Do you think we should move the money?" Cleon asked.

"To where? No, I think it's fine where it is. Let's get back to town before my nervous brother does something stupid."

He watched the two men walk away. He gave them some time, then broke from cover and went to the barn. He wanted to see if C.W. was inside.

The front doors were locked, and very solid, so he walked to the rear, hoping there was a back door. There was, and it was easily forced. Once inside, he lit a match. He was quickly able to tell that, although the team and wagon were there, the little Brit was not.

He went to the wagon, opened it, got in and checked the coffin. It was just as he had left it. He backed out of the barn, and headed to his hotel.

***

He slept fairly well that night, still with the chair beneath the doorknob and the gun by his side. In the morning he wondered if there was a decent place in town to get breakfast. When he got to the street, he remembered that he and C.W. had gone to a café between the hotel and the livery, so he went there, again. When he walked in there weren't many tables taken, but at one the sheriff was having breakfast.

"Mr. Adams," he called out. "Come and sit."

Clint thought, why not? He walked over and sat across from the man.

"Sir?" the waiter said.

"Ham-and-eggs, and coffee, please."

"Coming up."

"How was your night?" the lawman asked.

"You should know," Clint said. "You or your brother were watching my window the whole time."

"My brother," Sullivan said. "He can see a lot from his shop."

"So if Wellington had ridden in on his wagon, your brother would've seen him."

"Definitely."

The waiter brought Clint's breakfast quickly. He had the feeling it was because he was with the sheriff.

"I'm told this town is so quiet because of you," Clint said.

"I do my job."

"And if you have to go away for a while?" Clint asked. "Who do you leave in charge?"

"I never stay away very long," Sullivan said. "And everyone knows better than to get rowdy while I'm away."

"Have you heard about the spree of bank robberies in Wyoming?" Clint asked.

"I did hear about that," the sheriff said. "After all, that's my job."

"Are you worried about your town bank?"

"Our bank won't get hit," Sullivan said.

"Why not?"

"It's under my protection."

"What would you say if I told you I have a feeling that the traveling undertaker is involved?"

"That little weasel?" the sheriff asked. "Why would you say that?"

"Because," Clint said, "I think that wagon of his is a perfect hiding place for not only money, but the robbers themselves."

"Is that right?"

"Of course," Clint said, "that's just my opinion."

Sheriff Sullivan smiled at Clint and said, "Everybody's got one."

Chapter Thirty-Four

After breakfast, Clint felt it was time to get to it. If he waited for the Sullivan brothers to check the back of the wagon on their own, it might take forever. So he sat back in his chair and looked at the man.

"I think we should get to it, Sheriff," he said.

"Get to what?"

"The facts."

"And the facts are?" the man asked, with an innocent expression on his face.

"That you and your brother are robbing banks and using Caleb Wellington's wagon to hide the money bags."

"And how does that work?"

"You hit the bank, and at some point, before riding out of town, you toss the bags into the back of the wagon. The posse pursues you, but when they catch you, they find nothing."

"That's interestin'."

"And I think on at least one job, you and your partners probably hopped into the back of the wagon with the money, and C.W. just drove you out of town."

"What makes you think your traveling undertaker is part of this bank robbery gang?"

"He had to have a reason for shooting me," Clint said. "I think it was to get me out of the way."

"In case you haven't noticed," Sheriff Sullivan said, "I'm a lawman."

"And your brother's an undertaker," Clint said. "And after the job, you fellas come back here and do your jobs. Nobody's the wiser."

"Except you."

"Well, yes."

"And what makes you think you're right about this?" Sullivan asked.

"That's easy," Clint said. "The money."

"What about it?"

"I've got it."

Sullivan hesitated, then said, "What?"

"You left it in a coffin in the back of the wagon," Clint said. "It's not there, anymore."

Sullivan hesitated again, then smiled.

"You're bluffin'."

"You moved the wagon and the team twice," Clint said. "But that didn't matter. See, I removed the money while it was still in the barn."

Sullivan studied Clint for a few moments, then said, "You're a clever man, aren't you?"

"Usually," Clint said. "And this time, more clever than you."

Clint stood up and dropped some money onto the table.

"Breakfast is on me," he said, "since I think you're a little broke."

He walked out, leaving the lawman sitting there stiffly.

***

"He what?" Paul Sullivan said.

"He says he has our money."

Sheriff Sullivan had left the café after Clint and gone right to his brother's shop.

"He's bluffin'!"

"He says he got it while the wagon was still in the livery. He says he knows we've moved it twice."

"That sonofabitch!" Paul snapped. "How can we be sure?"

"That's easy," the sheriff said. "One of us has to go and look."

"One of us?" Paul asked. "You mean me?"

"No," the lawman said, "but I want you to go to the livery and tell Cleon to go and check it."

"Adams is gonna be watchin'."

"Yes, you and me," the sheriff said, "not Cleon."

"How can you be sure?"

"I can't," Tom Sullivan said, "but we have to know for sure whether or not he has our money."

"And if he does?" Paul asked.

"We'll have to kill 'im," Tom said, "but after we get our money back."

"And how are we gonna do that?"

"Easy," Tom said. "We're gonna trade for it."

"Trade?"

"Yeah," Sheriff Sullivan said. "If it's true, then he's got somethin' we want, and we've got somethin' he wants."

"What's that?"

"He doesn't give a damn about the money," Tom said. "He just wants the man who shot him."

"The little undertaker!" Paul said.

"Right."

"But what about—"

"Before we talk about it any further," the sheriff said, "let's find out if he's tellin' the truth. You go and tell Cleon to check, and then get back to me."

"Right."

As Paul started for the door his brother grabbed his arm and said, "Go out the back way."

Chapter Thirty-Five

Clint didn't bother watching them. He knew either the Sullivans, or Cleon would go to the wagon to check and see if he was bluffing. All he had to do was wait. He decided to do that in front of his hotel. He found a wooden chair in the lobby and brought it out to the porch. If he was the kind of man to whittle, he would have done so just to show how relaxed he was.

Maybe he should have brought Lemuel Gulliver out with him.

***

Cleon didn't like the idea, but he was the one who had to go and check the wagon.

"He's gonna be watchin' me and Tom," Paul explained. "Just go, take a look, and come right back."

"Do you really think he's got the money?" Cleon asked.

"That's what you're gonna find out," Paul said. "Now go! I'll wait for you here."

Cleon was not happy about going out to the wagon alone, but reluctantly left the livery.

***

Paul Sullivan nervously paced the inside of the livery, wondering if Clint Adams was outside, watching. He looked over at the Gunsmith's horse, standing calmly in a stall. Maybe they needed to have something else to trade for the money . . .

***

It suddenly occurred to Clint that he had left Eclipse in harm's way. Leaving the Darley in the livery was a bad idea. The Sullivans might decide, once they saw that he actually did have their money, that Eclipse would be good trade bait.

He stood up and quickly left the hotel porch.

***

When Cleon reached the old barn where they'd hidden the wagon, he looked around carefully. Clint Adams didn't seem to be around, so he approached the barn. He unlocked then swung the doors wide so he'd have enough light. The team of Clydesdale shifted nervously, not happy about having been left in the dark barn all night.

Cleon went to the back of the wagon and opened the door. He got a chill as he looked inside at the coffin. He didn't like the idea of this traveling undertaker, at all.

He climbed into the wagon, went to the coffin, and slowly lifted the heavy lid . . .

***

Paul Sullivan heard somebody approaching the livery. Since he couldn't be sure it was Cleon, he chose to hide. It was a good choice.

Clint Adams came walking in, went right to his horse's stall, backed him out, saddled him, and walked him off.

So much for trading the horse . . .

***

Clint walked Eclipse out of the livery and all the way back to the hotel. With the Darley safe and sound right in front of him, he went back to his chair to wait . . .

***

Cleon came staggering back into the livery, since he had run all the way.

"Paul!"

Paul Sullivan came out of hiding and said, "I had to take cover, because he came here."

"The Gunsmith?"

Paul nodded.

"He took his horse."

"That ain't all he took," Cleon said.

"It's gone?" Paul asked.

"It's gone," Cleon said. "All of it. That sonofabitch has our money."

Chapter Thirty-Six

Paul Sullivan and Cleon Jones entered the sheriff's office. Tom Sullivan looked up and didn't need either of them to say anything.

"Sonofabitch!" he swore.

"He's got it," Cleon said.

"The question is," Paul added, "what's he done with it?"

"That's simple," Tom said. "He's hidden it."

"Where?" Cleon asked.

"Did you look in the livery?" Tom asked.

Paul and Cleon exchanged a look.

"You didn't?"

"We came right here," Paul said.

"Well, go back there and tear that stable apart," the sheriff said. "We can't do anythin' until we know it's not there."

"Yeah, all right," Paul said.

"And what about his horse?" Tom asked. "Is it still there? We could always trade—"

"He thought of that," Paul said. "He came and got it."

"And where is he?" Tom asked.

"He's sittin' in front of the hotel," Paul said.

"Just sittin'!" Cleon said.

"Get back to that livery and find that money!"

***

Clint watched as Paul Sullivan and Cleon, the hostler, ran to the sheriff's office, then came out and ran back up the street, probably to the livery stable to search.

He only hoped he had hidden the bags well enough.

***

Sheriff Tom Sullivan walked to the front of his office and looked out the window. Sure enough. The Gunsmith was sitting in front of the hotel, looking very relaxed. And why not? The sonofabitch felt like he was in control. Somehow, the sheriff figured he had to take that away from him.

But how?

***

Paul and Cleon did as the sheriff told them to do, they tore the livery stable apart.

"It ain't here," Cleon said. "He hid it someplace else."

"But where?" Paul said. "He doesn't know the town like we do."

"Then those bags have gotta be in here," Cleon said, looking around.

"We're wastin' time," Paul said. "Let's get back to Tom. He's gotta have a plan, by now."

"Whatever his plan is," Cleon said, "we're gonna need help."

"I was thinkin' the same thing," Paul said. "Let's go."

They left the livery and ran back to the sheriff's office.

***

Clint watched the two men scurry back to the sheriff's office and smiled. So far, his plan was working perfectly. He was running them ragged!

***

Tom Sullivan looked up at his brother and Cleon as they entered again.

"Anythin'?" he asked.

"Nothin'," Paul said.

"Damn! Did you tear it apart like I told you?"

"Twice," Paul said.

"All right," the sheriff said, "that means I gotta go and talk to him."

"And see what he wants," Cleon added.

"We know what he wants," Tom said.

"Tom, me and Cleon think we might be needin' some help," Paul said.

"And for once in your life, big brother," the sheriff said, "you might be right."

"That ain't fair—" Paul started.

"Never mind," Tom said. "You and Cleon see who you can round up."

"What do we tell 'em?" Cleon asked.

"Tell 'em they stand to make a lot of money," Tom said, heading for the door.

"That's what we told 'em about the bank jobs," Paul said. "They're still waitin' to get paid."

"Then tell 'em about the Gunsmith," Tom said. "That'll either scare 'em out of town or get their interest."

"Should we tell 'em he's got our money?" Paul asked.

"Christ, no!" Tom snapped. "Tell 'em anythin' but that!"

Chapter Thirty-Seven

Sheriff Tom Sullivan came out of his office and walked slowly across the street toward Clint. Finally, Clint thought, they were going to get to some negotiating. Although he *had* enjoyed watching Paul Sullivan and Cleon run back and forth.

Sheriff Sullivan paused a moment to look Eclipse over, then stepped up onto the porch.

"That's quite an animal," the lawman said.

"Don't even think about it," Clint said.

"What?"

"If you threaten my horse, or injure him in any way, I'll kill you where you stand," Clint said. "I won't care about the money, or that little Brit undertaker."

"Whoa, take it easy, there, Adams," the lawman said. "I ain't threatenin' your horse, just admirin' it."

"I suppose you know by now that I wasn't bluffing," Clint said. "Your brother told you the money's gone."

"You seem to have most of this figured out," Tom Sullivan said.

"What am I missing?" Clint asked. "You and your brother—probably Cleon, or a few others—rob banks, hide the money in the wagon, and then come back here."

"You're missin' your little friend, Wellington," the sheriff said. "You want him, don't you?"

"I do."

"Are you willin' to trade the money for him?"

"Maybe," Clint said.

"What else would you want?"

"I'd have to see C.W., and talk to him, before I decide on that trade."

"You want me to let you see him *before* you give me the money?"

"That's right."

Sheriff Sullivan looked stunned.

"I can't do that."

"You don't have to give him to me," Clint said, "just let me talk to him."

Tom Sullivan rubbed his jaw.

"I'm gonna have to think about that."

"Take your time," Clint said. "I'm in no hurry. How much money is in those bags, anyway?"

"Never mind," Sullivan said. "I've got other partners I've gotta talk to."

"Oh, come now," Clint said. "I know you call the shots, Sheriff."

"That may be," Sullivan said, "but I still can't make all the decisions on my own. Not when it comes to money."

"Well then, go and talk to them," Clint said. "I'm very comfortable right here."

"You look it."

"But I'll tell you this," Clint said. "If anybody starts shooting, all bets are off. I'll just do what I do best."

"I know," Sheriff Sullivan said. "Kill people."

Clint let it go without comment. The sheriff turned and walked back to his office.

***

When Sullivan entered his office, it was empty. Paul and Cleon were out trying to roundup some help. They weren't going to be able to make a move on the Gunsmith unless they had enough guns.

And since they didn't have enough good guns, they needed to gather many guns.

He sat behind his desk to wait.

***

Clint hadn't seen the undertaker and hostler come out of the sheriff's office, but he suspected they might have been instructed by the sheriff to start using the back door.

No matter what happened, there was no way Clint was going to allow the Sullivan brothers to keep the bank money. But he also wasn't about to let Caleb Wellington get away with shooting him. So he was in an all or nothing situation. On top of that, his shoulder was stiff, so he kept flexing his right hand to keep it as loose as possible.

He had gotten himself into a position where he might end up taking on a whole town. Luckily, the town didn't look like it was loaded with guns.

It remained to be seen just how many men Sheriff Sullivan could muster against him.

***

Paul Sullivan came in the back door of the office, without Cleon.

"What's wrong?" the sheriff asked.

"The boys we've been usin' for our bank jobs ain't happy, Tom."

"Whataya mean?"

"They want their shares," Paul said, "and they don't wanna go up against the Gunsmith."

"Where's Cleon?"

"He's still askin'," Paul said. "We'll get some men, Tom, but not enough. Did you talk to him?"

"Yes."

"Will you trade?"

"He wants to see the traveling undertaker and talk to him, first," the sheriff said.

"What did you tell 'im?"

"That I had to think about it, and talk to my partners," Tom said.

"What partners?"

"You, ya idiot."

"Oh, so now that we hafta go up against the Gunsmith I'm a partner, huh?"

"We're all in this together, Paul," Tom said to his brother.

"That may be so, Tom," Paul said, "but it's still you givin' the orders, ain't it?"

"That's right, I am," Tom said. "So you go out the back door, find Cleon, and you two get me some men!"

"Yeah, right."

"And try and make it somebody who knows one end of a gun from the other!" he called out.

Chapter Thirty-Eight

Sherriff Tom Sullivan looked at the men assembled in his office. His brother Paul and Cleon had brought in four others. Two of those were men they had used on bank jobs. The other two were guns for hire who liked the idea of getting a reputation for killing the Gunsmith.

"When do we go?" Paul asked.

"I'm still gonna try a trade," Sheriff Sullivan said. "He wants that little undertaker Wellington, we're gonna give him to 'im."

"We?" Paul asked.

"You and me, Paul," Sullivan said. "Right now. Let's go."

"Why don't we just all go and get it over with?" Paul asked.

"Because he's still got our money, that's why," Tom said. "After we get the money, he's open game."

The four newcomers seemed to like that idea.

"Cleon, you stay here with the boys," Tom said.

"I got no problem with that," the hostler said.

"Come on, Paul," Tom said.

***

Clint watched as the two Sullivan brothers came out of the sheriff's office and crossed the street to him.

"All right, Adams," the sheriff said, "you can have it your way."

"Spell it out for me," Clint said.

"We'll take you to Wellington," Tom said. "After you see him, you'll give us our money."

Clint stood.

"Let's go. How far is it?"

"Not far," Tom said. "We can walk."

"If you don't mind," Clint said, grabbing Eclipse's reins, "I'm going to keep my horse with me. Lead the way." He was still concerned that they might try to use Eclipse's safety against him. If it came to it, he'd actually give up the money and the traveling undertaker for that horse.

Paul was nervous, but Tom seemed calm. The two Sullivans walked ahead of him, and Clint followed, mindful that someone might be coming up behind him. But they wouldn't want to backshoot him until they had their money.

They walked him to the edge of town, past the livery and out of town. Clint suddenly knew where they were going.

"The cemetery?" he asked.

"Where else would you expect to find an undertaker?" Sheriff Sullivan asked.

"Not that it's much of a cemetery," Paul added. "Folks around here don't want a boot hill in town. They usually bury their loved ones near home."

"Are you telling me that Caleb Wellington is buried here?" Clint asked. "You killed him?"

When they reached the small cemetery with just a few grave markers, the sheriff turned to face Clint.

"We wanted his wagon and team. We recruited him, but when he came back and told us that he shot you, that wasn't what we expected. We asked if you were dead, and he said he didn't know. I'd had enough of him, by then."

"So you killed him."

Sheriff Sullivan shrugged.

"It seemed the easiest way to go."

"Which one is his?"

"That one." Paul Sullivan pointed to a grave that looked freshly filled in.

"Well," Clint said, "dig him up."

"What?" Paul said.

"Now wait—" Tom started.

"You don't expect me to take your word for it that he's in there, do you?" Clint asked. "He shot me. If he's dead, I want to see him."

"Look here—" Paul started.

"All right," Tom said, cutting his brother off, "we'll dig him up. He ain't planted that far down, anyway."

Tom looked around, then pointed to one side where two shovels were sticking up out of the dirt.

"Get those, Paul," Tom said. "Let's do this."

Chapter Thirty-Nine

It didn't take long for the two brothers to dig up the coffin. It was a cheap pine box, not one of the fine ones C.W. had in his wagon.

They didn't bother lifting it up out of the grave.

"Open it," Clint ordered.

Tom looked at his brother and said, "Open it, Paul."

Paul got down into the hole, pried up the lid of the coffin with the edge of a shovel, and then stepped back as if fell off. Lying in the box, with his hands crossed over his chest, was the little Brit traveling undertaker, Caleb Wellington. Clint could see he'd been shot in the chest.

"Satisfied?" Tom asked.

"Yes," Clint said. "Cover him up."

"We can do that later—"

"No," Clint said, "now. Bury him again, and then meet me at my hotel and we'll talk."

Instead of walking back to the hotel, Clint mounted Eclipse and rode off. He had to have his next move all mapped out by the time they joined him.

***

Clint needed help, somebody to watch his back, and he could only think of one man to do it. He could have just kept riding, left the money hidden and let the Sullivan brothers tear the whole town apart trying to find it. But that would've left unfinished business, and he hated that. So he rode back to the hotel and took his seat in front, to wait.

***

The Sullivan brothers finished planting the little undertaker again and tossed the shovels aside.

"Damn him for makin' us do that," Paul said, brushing the dirt off his clothes.

"Well, he got what he wanted," Tom said. "Now let's go get what we want."

"Alone?" Paul asked. "I mean . . . just the two of us?"

"No," Tom said, "we'll bring some help . . ."

***

Clint watched as the sheriff, his brother, Cleon, and four other men left the sheriff's office and crossed over to him. It was time.

When they reached the hotel they spread out, while Tom Sullivan stepped up onto the porch.

"Where's our money, Adams?" Tom asked.

"Did I say I had your money?" Clint asked.

"You did," Tom said. "Don't play games with us."

"I don't like games, Sheriff," Clint said. "I think you should have somebody bring that wagon and team here."

"Those belong to us," Tom said. "We earned them."

"By killing Caleb Wellington?" Clint asked. "That's not earning, that's stealing."

"Whatever you wanna call it, they're ours," Tom said.

"Well, have them brought here, anyway," Clint said. "I don't want them, I just want to look at them."

"Are you tellin' me the money's in the wagon?" Tom asked, "You hid the bags there, and my brother and Cleon couldn't find them?"

"Just have them brought here," Clint said, "and we'll see."

Tom studied Clint, then turned to Cleon and said, "Take two men. Bring the wagon and team here." Then he looked at Clint. "We'll wait here with you."

"Be my guest."

***

They could all hear the sound of the wagon approaching and watched as it appeared on the street. As it came to a halt in front of the hotel, they moved.

172

Cleon set the reins aside, and he and the other two men stepped down.

"There," Tom Sullivan said. "As you asked. Now, where's the money?"

Clint looked around at the seven men facing him, all armed.

"This is quite a show of force, Sheriff," he said.

"Well," Tom said, "you *are* the Gunsmith."

"That may be, but seven men is a lot, even for me," Clint told him.

"Then talk," Tom said, "or you'll see seven men drawing their guns."

"I don't think so."

"Why not?"

"Do you really think I'd be foolish enough to come here alone, with no one to watch my back?"

"I don't see anybody," Tom said.

"But he sees you."

"What?"

"My man has a rifle pointed at you at this very minute," Clint said.

"One man with a rifle?" Tom asked. "He'd never get us before we get you."

"Maybe not," Clint said, "but he'll get you, Sheriff. Anybody draws a weapon, and you won't see the outcome."

Tom Sullivan kept his eyes on Clint's.

"You're bluffing."

"I don't bluff," Clint said.

Tom looked up and down the street, and at the roof-tops.

"Where is he?" Tom asked. "Who is he?"

"He's where he can see you, but you can't see him," Clint said, in a tone so low only the sheriff could hear him.

Again, the sheriff scanned the street and rooftops.

"Who?" he asked.

"A man who's an expert with a rifle," Clint said. "He'll put a bullet in you with no trouble."

"One man?" Tom asked, "You brought one man to back your play?"

"Believe me," Clint said, "Lemuel Gulliver is the only man I need."

Chapter Forty

Clint could only hope that none of the men were readers. If they were not, then he was putting Jonathan Swift's creation to good use.

"Gulliver," Tom said. "I don't know the name."

"You wouldn't."

Clint could see Sullivan's mind working. Then his brother, Paul, stepped up beside him.

"What's the hold up?"

"He has a man somewhere here in town with a rifle," Tom said. "It's pointed at me."

"Where?" Paul demanded, looking around.

"I don't know," Tom said, "but he said a name—Gulliver, Lemuel Gulliver."

"Do you know him?"

"No." Tom grabbed Paul's arm. "Go back to my office. All the wanted posters are in the desk. Go through them, see if you find a Lemuel Gulliver."

"How do you spell it?"

"I don't know," Tom said. "Just see what you can find out."

"Should I take somebody with me?" Paul asked.

"Sure, take Cleon."

As Paul and Cleon headed back to the office, Clint studied the other five. Tom Sullivan would be the one he took first. He'd have to study the other four a bit longer before he assigned them a number. If they went for their guns now, he'd just have to improvise.

"Why don't you have a seat?" Clint asked.

"Aren't you afraid that would take me out of your man's reach?"

"No," Clint said, "he's very efficient. There are more chairs in the lobby."

The sheriff went inside, came back with a chair, set it down about six feet from Clint and sat. He could've shot Clint in the back from the lobby, but that wouldn't have gotten him the money. He also could've kept going and gotten away from Adams and his Gulliver, but that wouldn't have gotten him the money, either.

"So tell me," Clint said, "how did you recruit C.W.?"

"Wellington? Yeah, he liked to be called that, didn't he?" Tom said.

"Yes."

"Well," Tom said, "when the two of you came here and I saw that wagon, I got the idea of using it."

"To rob banks."

"Sure, why not?"

"Did you ever think about robbing your own bank?" Clint asked.

"That's been closed a while," Tom said. "There's nothin' there."

"I see. So are you robbing other town's banks so you can replenish your own?"

"Nothin' so noble," Tom Sullivan said. "We're robbin' banks to make money for ourselves."

"At least you're honest about it."

They looked over at the four men in the street, two shuffling their feet nervously, the other two standing still. Clint dubbed the two standing still One and Two, the order in which he'd kill them if the time came.

After Tom Sullivan, of course.

"My brother went to talk to Wellington, made the mistake of talkin' to you first."

"Then when he left my room, he did go and talk to C.W.," Clint said.

"That's right, to recruit him."

"And he came on board?"

"Apparently," Tom said, "things hadn't been goin' so well for him since he came to this country. The money we offered appealed to him."

"All he had to do was get rid of me."

"Well," Tom said, "we didn't tell him to kill you, but yeah."

So shooting Clint was a spur of moment reaction by Caleb Wellington. Well, maybe knowing that he wouldn't have killed him, but that point was moot, since the man was already dead.

"You know," Tom Sullivan said, "you *could* have your man Gulliver take a shot, just to prove he's there."

"I could," Clint said, and left it at that.

Chapter Forty-One

While he was waiting, it suddenly occurred to Clint that there was another question to be asked.

"Did you kill Jake Lamb before or after C.W.?" he said to Tom Sullivan.

"What?" Sheriff Sullivan asked. "Who?"

"He looked like a mountain man, wore buckskins," Clint said.

"Oh, him," Tom Sullivan asked. "Where the hell did he come from? He appeared in town just before one of our robberies, started asking questions about the wagon. We had no choice."

"You always have a choice when it comes to killing a man," Clint said. "For instance, I could choose to raise my hand now and have you shot dead."

"Look, if that old mountain man was a friend of yours—"

"He was," Clint said. "I don't mind that you killed C.W., but you didn't have to kill Jake."

"Hey, look," the lawman said, "I never wanted to kill anybody. All I wanted to do was pull a few bank jobs and put some money away for my retirement. Then you got involved, and your mountain man friend, and your stupid traveling undertaker—what made him think that idea was going to work?"

"He was desperate," Clint said. "He left his country, came here to make his fortune and it didn't happen."

"Anybody coulda told 'im that," Sullivan said.

***

Across the street, in the sheriff's office, Paul and Cleon were going through the wanted posters, trying to find anything with the name Lemuel Gulliver on it.

"There's nothin' here," Cleon finally said.

"That don't mean he ain't out there with a rifle," Paul Sullivan pointed out. "It just means he ain't wanted."

"So what now?"

"I got an idea," Paul said. "I'll go across the street and talk with Tom. You go to the hotel, go to Adams' room, and see if you can find anything about this Gulliver."

"All right," Cleon said. "Let's go."

"Go out the back here," Paul said, "and in the back door of the hotel."

"Got it."

"Let's go.

***

180

Once again, Clint watched as Paul Sullivan came across the street. His brother, Tom, got up from the chair and met him halfway, so Clint couldn't hear their conversation. Eventually, Tom turned and walked back to Clint.

"Looks like your man ain't wanted," he said.

"I never said he was. I just said he was good with a rifle."

"I still think you're bluffin'," Tom said.

"Then why don't you have your men draw on me," Clint asked him, "and then we'll see if you're around for what happens next."

"Nobody's drawin' on anybody until we get our money," Tom said. "It ain't in this wagon, because we've been all through it. And it ain't in the livery stable. So tell me, Adams, where is it?"

"You know," Clint said, "I'm kind of ashamed that, up until a few minutes ago, I forgot about poor Jake Lamb."

"Again? That old mountain man got in the way, Adams. Live with it."

"Oh, I *am* going to have to live with it" Clint said. "Tell me, who actually cut his throat?"

"Paul's our undertaker," Tom said, "and he's pretty good with a knife."

Clint looked over at Paul, who was still standing in the empty street. The other four men were spread out, although two of them were over by the large wagon. The Clydesdales were standing very still, as was Eclipse. There was a lot of tension in the air, and Clint knew that, at some point, things were going to have to explode. He was still surprised that, in a town this size, there were no onlookers.

"Where is everybody?" Clint asked.

"Whataya mean?"

"This is a fair-sized town," Clint said. "Where are all the people?"

"I told you, the bank closed," Sullivan said. "After that, people started movin' away."

"So it's actually a ghost town?"

"Pretty near."

"You're the sheriff of a ghost town?"

"Looks like it, don't it?"

"Were you voted in?"

"Hell, no," Tom said, "I walked into the sheriff's office, the badge was on the desk, and I put it on."

Clint never liked exchanging shots with a lawman. Now it was obvious that wasn't going to be the case. Tom Sullivan was not an actual lawman.

"So what are we waitin;' for?" Tom asked. "You've seen Wellington, you've seen the wagon and team, and you've got your man with his rifle pointed at me. Give us the money and ride out."

"I want to do that," Clint said, "but somehow, I just can't."

"Adams—" Tom started, but at that point Cleon came out of the hotel, holding something in his hand. He went over to Tom and handed it to him.

Tom Sullivan stared down at it, then examined it more thoroughly. He then looked at Clint and tossed the copy of *Gulliver's Travels* into his lap.

The jig was up.

Chapter Forty-Two

"Lemuel Gulliver?" Tom asked.

Clint shrugged.

"It seemed like a good joke, at the time."

"So there's nobody out here pointing a rifle at me," the self-appointed lawman said.

"Sheriff, I don't need to have anybody pointing a rifle at you," Clint said. "No matter what happens here, no matter who draws first, you're going to be the first one I kill. It's as simple as that."

Clint put the book down next to his chair.

Tom Sullivan stared at him, and Clint could see his mind working.

"Are you fast enough to do that?" Tom finally asked.

"There's one way to find out," Clint told him.

"So if I get up from this chair and walk out into the street—"

"There's no getting up from that chair," Clint said. "If you do, I'll kill you."

"And then they'll kill you," Tom said.

"And neither one of us will be around to see if they finally find the money."

"You're frustratin' the hell out of me, Adams," Sullivan said. "It might be worth it knowin' that you'll be dead, too."

"Then go ahead," Clint said, "give the word. Let's do it."

"Where is my money!" Tom Sullivan screamed, leaning forward in his chair.

It didn't startle Clint, but it did startle the men standing in the street.

"Easy, Tom," Clint said. "They almost went for their guns."

"Nobody draws unless I do," Tom yelled at his men.

They all looked at each other and moved their hands away from their guns. Clint knew he had Tom where he wanted him, because in spite of his frustration, the man didn't get out of his chair.

"Adams," Tom said, "we can't sit here like this all day."

"No," Clint said, "you're right, we can't. I'll tell you what. When you took me to the cemetery, it wasn't the first time I'd been there."

"Whataya talkin' about?"

"Send some of your boys there to dig up a few graves," Clint suggested.

"You buried the money?"

"And while I was there, I should've noticed that new grave you showed me. I mean, I was almost standing on top of it."

Tom called his brother Paul over.

"You and Cleon go on over to the cemetery and dig up every grave around that little undertaker's."

"He buried the money?" Paul asked.

"Just go!"

The two men ran off.

"Adams," Tom said, "if they don't find the money, I'll have to forget about it, and we're gonna have us a blood bath."

***

While they were waiting, Clint couldn't help thinking back on how this whole mess started. C.W.'s idea of putting him in one of his coffins still made no sense to him. And the little undertaker shooting him made even less sense. But he couldn't ask him about either one of those things, because he was dead and buried.

"I've got a question," he said to Tom.

"Go ahead," Sullivan said. "We've got time."

"How did it first start?" Clint asked. "I mean, did you offer to buy C.W.'s wagon and team, or just recruit him right away?"

"I had Paul recruit 'im," Tom said. "I thought the whole package—him, the wagon, the team, the traveling undertaker dodge—would work well. And who would suspect him of being involved with the robberies?"

"Nobody."

"Exactly."

"And he went for it right away?"

"Like I said before," Tom said, "he liked the money we were talkin' about."

"Yeah, I guess he did."

Clint was tempted to reach down, pick up *Gulliver's Travels* and start reading it, but was afraid that might push Tom Sullivan over the edge.

***

Before long Paul and Cleon came back, looking bedraggled and dirty, but empty handed.

Paul stepped up onto the porch and said to his brother," He lied. The money ain't there."

Tom looked at Clint and growled, "Adams—"

"Now wait a second, Sheriff," Clint said. "Think about it. I put the money there. Somebody's lying, but it's not me."

Tom looked at Paul, and then out into the street at Cleon.

"Did you and Cleon stay together or split up?" he asked.

"We split up," Paul said. "There were too many graves."

"And Cleon said he didn't find the money?"

"Yeah," Paul drawled, slowly, "that's what he *said*."

They both looked out at Cleon, who was talking to two of the other men.

Chapter Forty-Three

Clint saw Tom Sullivan glance down at the book at Clint's feet, and knew he'd lost the man.

"No," the lawman said to Paul, "Cleon's not smart enough for that." He looked at Clint. "That's not gonna work, Adams. You've already bluffed us enough."

Tom started to get up, but his brother put his hand on his shoulder to hold him in place.

"We need that money, Tom."

"We kill him," Tom said, pointing at Clint, "we go and get more money."

"And what if he kills you?" Paul asked. "You're the leader, little brother."

"Look at him," Tom said. "I want to wipe that smug look off his face."

"Yeah," Paul said, "but I want you to see that happen."

With that, Paul suddenly turned toward Clint with a gun in his hand. He must have picked it up at some point when he was in the sheriff's office. Clint had no choice but to draw and fire, sending a bullet into Paul's chest.

"Get him!" Tom shouted.

Paul had fallen back into his brother's embrace, which meant Tom was shielded. Clint had no choice as all the other men drew their weapons. He flipped over backward in his chair and rolled into the lobby of the hotel before getting to his feet.

With Paul Sullivan dead, that still left six men with guns on the street, and that was too many even for the Gunsmith to face.

He continued on through the lobby, past the startled desk clerk, through the back door of the hotel and out.

The rest of this was going to take place on the streets of Venture, but not head on.

***

Tom Sullivan lowered his brother's body to the ground. Then he held his hand out to the other five men, who started to charge the front door of the hotel, with intentions of following Clint Adams.

"Stop!" he shouted.

Cleon and the others stopped and stared at him.

"We've let him call the play long enough," Tom said. "Now it's our turn."

"And how do we do that?" Cleon asked.

"We've got his horse," Tom said. "Cleon, take the animal to the stable and watch him. If and when the time comes, you'll be the one to put a bullet between the horse's eyes."

Cleon was appalled. Kill that magnificent animal?

"But Tom—"

"You heard me!" Tom said. "Grab it!"

Cleon turned and looked at the Gunsmith's horse. There was no way he could see himself killing this animal. Not for any reason.

He walked toward Eclipse as the other men awaited their orders from the sheriff.

***

As Clint came out the back door of the hotel, he cursed himself for having to leave Eclipse out front. His only hope was that the Darley had run after he fired the shot that killed Paul Sullivan. Because, if push ever came to shove, he'd give up his life to save his horse.

***

"Take my brother's body over to his shop," Tom told two of the men. "Put him on one of the tables, and then get back here."

"Right," one of them said. He and another man lifted the body and carried it away.

"What about us?" one of the other men asked.

Tom looked at the two men still in front of him. These were the two who could actually handle a gun. He gave the three of them—himself included—a more than even chance against the Gunsmith.

"We're gonna kill 'im, when he comes for his horse."

At that moment Tom looked over at Eclipse, who reared up onto his hind legs with a loud squeal, then turned and ran off down the street.

"Damn you, Cleon!"

"I couldn't help it," Cleon lied. "He just went crazy."

In actuality, Cleon had done whatever he could to get the horse to run. In the end, he yanked on the reins so that the horse's bit would cause him enough pain to get him to rear. After that, the horse's instincts took over, and he ran.

***

From where Clint was, he heard Eclipse scream, but didn't hear a shot. Hopefully, whatever had caused the horse pain had not been fatal.

He moved away from the hotel, figuring his best move at that moment was to head for the money.

Chapter Forty-Four

He went back to the stable, where he'd first found the money. When he first took the money bags from the wagon, he'd looked around for a place to hide them. That was when he came across the small cemetery. He saw the shovels and briefly considered burying the bags in one of the graves. But that would've meant digging up some poor soul's grave, and he didn't want to do that. So he left the cemetery but took a shovel with him. Somewhere between the cemetery and the barn, he found a shallow area that looked as if it had once been a waterhole but had dried up. It seemed a likely place to hide the bags, as he didn't need to dig, just set them down and cover them. He had done that, first with dirt, then with some loose foliage.

Now he went back to the cemetery, grabbed one of the shovels and took it with him. When he found the shallow spot where he'd covered the money, it looked undisturbed. He removed the foliage and dirt with the shovel and reclaimed the three bags of money. They were from three different banks. The one from Cody was the heaviest.

The question was, what to do with them now?

***

When the two men returned from the undertaker's shop Tom Sullivan said, "We're gonna find him. And the money."

"How?" Cleon asked.

"We should split up," one of the men said.

"We are," Tom said, "but in two groups of three. Cleon, you take those two. Put that wagon and team back in your barn. You two come with me."

"Where do we look?" Cleon asked. "After we stow the wagon?"

"All over," Tom said. "You three start with the hotel. My group will start at the cemetery."

"Believe me, boss," Cleon said, "we didn't find the money there."

"We're just gonna use it as a startin' point," Tom said.

"What do we do if we find 'im?" Cleon asked.

"If he has the money, take it and kill 'im," Tom said. "If you find him and he doesn't have the money, kill 'im."

"We shoulda killed him where he sat in front of the hotel," Cleon said. "Instead of lettin' him call the tune."

"You're right, we should've," Tom said. "My brother's dead because of my bad judgment, and that's on me.

That's why when we find him, money or not, we're gonna kill 'im. Understand?"

"I understand, Sheriff," Cleon said.

The two groups of three went their separate ways.

***

Clint heard the wagon coming, watched from cover while Cleon and two other men drove it into the barn, then closed the doors and left. What better place to hide the money than someplace they had already looked?

He went into the barn through the back door, then inside the wagon. He put the money bags back in the coffin he had originally taken them from, not particularly caring if they were found or not. When this was all over, if he was still alive, he'd get the money back to the banks. If not . . . well, he figured, so be it.

***

When Tom Sullivan and the two men he had dubbed One and Two got to the cemetery, they looked around briefly.

"What are we lookin' for?" One asked.

"It's not what we're lookin' for," Tom said, pointing, "it's what's missin'."

He noticed where there had been two shovels, there was now only one.

"He's around here, somewhere," Tom said. "Split up. When you spot him, sing out. Don't try to take 'im."

One and Two exchanged a look, but then they moved out.

Tom Sullivan put his hands on his hips, then decided to head for the livery stable. Halfway there, he found the second shovel and the shallow area where something had obviously been hidden.

He went back to the cemetery to collect One and Two.

"Come with me," he said.

"You find 'im?" One asked.

"No, but I know what direction he went. Follow me."

***

Clint figured they'd split up to try to find him. He also figured he could pick them off that way. But he doubted the six of them would go off by themselves. It was more likely they'd search in twos or threes.

Clint also figured they'd be looking for him all through town. He decided—since he now knew the place was basically a ghost town—to go and meet them, head on.

Chapter Forty-Five

Of course, his plan to meet them head on depended on the men having split up into groups—hopefully pairs, maybe threes. He intended to head back toward the center of town, where the hotel, the sheriff's office and the undertaker's shop were all located. But before he did that, he walked up the slope to where he had left Eclipse when he first arrived. Sure enough, the Darley, looking for someplace familiar to wait, was there.

"Thank God you're smart," Clint said, stroking the Darley's neck, then he checked him for injuries and found none. "And healthy."

He left the horse there once again, untethered, so he'd be able to run off if the need arose, and head back to town.

***

Cleon and his two men searched the hotel and came up empty. No money, and no Gunsmith.

When they came back out the front door, Cleon saw the book and picked it up.

"Gulliver's Travels," he said, reading the title. "I wonder what this is about?"

"What does it matter?" one of the men said. "You ain't never read a book before."

Cleon was about to answer when someone said, "Excuse me, that's mine."

All three men turned toward the voice . . .

***

Clint was across the street in front of the undertaker's shop when he saw Cleon come out of the hotel with two men. Luckily, they found something to attract their attention, and he was able to cross the street unobserved.

When he got within earshot and saw that they were looking at his book, he said, "Excuse me, that's mine."

As the three men turned to look at him, they all went for their guns.

***

As Tom Sullivan, along with One and Two, were approaching the livery stable, the self-appointed lawman saw a shovel leaning against the wall.

"Damn," he said, but then they all heard the volley of shots coming from town.

"Let's go!" he shouted.

***

When they reached the hotel, they saw the three bodies lying on the front porch. The chair Sullivan and Clint Adams had been sitting in were overturned, and the copy of *Gulliver's Travels* was gone.

Sullivan stepped up and checked Cleon and the other two men.

"They're dead," he said.

"They were useless with guns," One said. "He won't take the three of us that easy."

"He won't take us at all," Tom said, "if we can find that money before we find him."

"Where do you figure?" Two asked.

"He dug it up from where he hid it," Tom said.

"And put it where?" Two asked.

Tom Sullivan looked up and down the street, thinking for a moment.

"Where's the best place to hide somethin'?" he asked.

"Where?" Two asked.

Tom smiled.

"Where someone has already looked. Come on!"

He took off toward the stable again, with One and Two close on his heels.

***

When they got into the stable Tom said to One and Two, "You watch the front doors, you watch the back."

"Gotcha," both men said.

As they took up their positions, Tom went to the wagon and climbed up into the back. Everything there looked undisturbed, including the heavy coffin in the center. He knelt next to it and lifted the lid. Sure enough, the clever Gunsmith had outsmarted himself, and put the money bags right back where he'd first stolen them from.

Tom looked inside each bag, to make sure the cash was still there. Then he closed the lid. Was there any way he could take this money without the other two men knowing about it? He'd been willing to split with his brother, Paul, but had all along been trying to figure a way to cut the other men out. Now some of them were dead, and the last two were there with him.

It was too bad he couldn't figure out a way to have the Gunsmith kill them while he got away.

Chapter Forty-Six

After taking care of Cleon and his two men, Clint took cover and waited for Tom Sullivan and the other two to arrive. Since Tom had told him earlier that Paul could see everything from his window, that's where he went, into the undertaker's shop. It didn't bother him that Paul Sullivan was lying on a table, there.

He watched as Tom checked the bodies, and while he watched he held his copy of *Gulliver's Travels* in his left hand. But he set it down, with intentions of picking it up later. But then he saw Tom Sullivan and his two men start running. It seemed to him they were headed for the stable.

He left the shop and followed.

***

Tom decided he had to play it straight for his men, at least for now.

"The money's here!" he called, leaning out the back of the wagon.

"Whatta we do now?" One asked, from the front doors.

"We get outta here," Tom said. "Do you two have horses in here?"

"No," Two said, "we keep them somewhere else."

"Well, grab two of these and saddle them," Tom said. "I'll take the wagon."

"You're gonna leave town?" Two asked.

"I'm pretty much done here," Tom Sullivan said.

"But you're the sheriff," One said.

Tom took the badge off his shirt and tossed it into the dirt.

"Not anymore."

***

Clint approached the stable, heard voices from inside. He knew they had to be watching both the front and back doors. So rather than force his way in, he decided to wait for them to come out, which they'd have to do, eventually.

He didn't have to wait long. Soon he heard the two large front doors creak and watched as they swung open.

He got ready.

***

"We're gonna ride out," Tom said, "and keep goin'."

"What if he's out there?" One asked.

"You fellas want a crack at the Gunsmith, don't you?" Tom asked.

"We do," Two said.

"If we got out on the run, we'll be able to take 'im," Tom predicted. Although he had no intention of trying to help them. He was coming out of the stable hell-bent-for-leather.

Let's see what these big, strong horses can do, he thought.

***

Clint spread his legs, planted his feet and readied himself. The doors opened and first two men on horses rode out at a full gallop. Following them came the wagon pulled by the Clydesdales, with Tom Sullivan whipping them into a frenzy.

The first two men came out shooting, even before they saw Clint standing there. But he held his ground as the two horsemen rode at him. Meanwhile, Tom Sullivan turned the wagon and drove it out of town.

Clint remained calm. He knew the Clydesdales would not be able to keep up that pace. They were not built for speed.

He drew his gun and fired twice. Each man was tugged off his horse as if jerked from behind. The horses continued on and ran to either side of Clint.

He walked to the fallen men, checked to be sure they were dead, then began walking to where he'd left Eclipse.

***

Tom Sullivan kept whipping the Clydesdales but couldn't get them past a certain speed. He thought they could probably run all day, and that was all he thought he needed. But he soon found he was wrong, when he saw a rider up ahead, just sitting on his horse, waiting for him. As he got closer, he saw that it was Clint Adams. With that Darley Arabian of his, he'd been able to get ahead of Sullivan and the wagon and wait.

Sullivan considered trying to ride over him, but the Gunsmith would be too smart for that. Obviously, Sullivan had no men left, and Clint Adams could simply wait for the Clydesdales to run out of steam. Stupid goddamn thick horses would never be able to outrun or outlast that Darley.

Sullivan reined in the team and stopped, stared at Clint Adams.

"My men all dead?" he asked.

"Every one of them."

"And the money is in this wagon," Sullivan said. "We can share it."

"I don't think so," Clint said. "I think you killed Jake Lamb, Sullivan."

"And his life is worth this money?" Sullivan asked.

"And more."

Tom Sullivan stood up and set the team's reins aside.

"Then I guess this ends one way," Sullivan said.

"It was always going to," Clint said.

They both went for their guns, only Tom Sullivan's never cleared leather. Clint's bullet took him right off the seat of the wagon and dumped him onto the ground.

Clint rode Eclipse right up to the Clydesdales, and he spoke to them until they calmed down. Then he climbed into the wagon to make sure the money was still there. He decided he would not bring the money back to each bank that was robbed. He would simply take it all to the Bank of Cody and let them send the other banks their share.

He moved forward to the seat of the large wagon, picked up the reins and started the Clydesdales forward at a more reasonable pace, with Eclipse following behind.

Coming July 27, 2020

THE GUNSMITH
461
Standoff in Labyrinth

For more information
visit: www.SpeakingVolumes.us

On Sale Now!

THE GUNSMITH
459
The Imperial Crown

For more information
visit: www.SpeakingVolumes.us

On Sale Now!

TALBOT ROPER NOVELS
by
ROBERT J. RANDISI

On Sale Now!

Lady Gunsmith
Books 1 - 8
Roxy Doyle and the Silver Queen

On Sale!

Award-Winning Author
Robert J. Randisi (J.R. Roberts)

For more information
visit: www.SpeakingVolumes.us